UNLEASHED

SPEAK EVIL

Ali Sparkes
UNLEASHED

SPEAK EVIL

OXFORD
UNIVERSITY PRESS

OXFORD
UNIVERSITY PRESS

Great Clarendon Street, Oxford OX2 6DP

Oxford University Press is a department of the University of Oxford.
It furthers the University's objective of excellence in research, scholarship,
and education by publishing worldwide in

Oxford New York

Auckland Cape Town Dar es Salaam Hong Kong Karachi
Kuala Lumpur Madrid Melbourne Mexico City Nairobi
New Delhi Shanghai Taipei Toronto

With offices in

Argentina Austria Brazil Chile Czech Republic France Greece
Guatemala Hungary Italy Japan Poland Portugal Singapore
South Korea Switzerland Thailand Turkey Ukraine Vietnam

Oxford is a registered trade mark of Oxford University Press
in the UK and in certain other countries

British Library Cataloguing in Publication Data

Data available

ISBN: 978-0-19-275609-1

1 3 5 7 9 10 8 6 4 2

Printed in Great Britain

Paper used in the production of this book is a natural,
recyclable product made from wood grown in sustainable forests.
The manufacturing process conforms to the environmental
regulations of the country of origin.

To the real Jacob and Alex,
with limitless love.

A Port in a Storm

He knew he was in for it as soon as he heard the key. One . . . two . . . three attempts, the metal scratching the paint, and a rising growl of indistinct curses, before the chink of acceptance in the lock.

He eyed the rain-spattered window. Was it worth the drop? Last time he'd sprained his ankle badly.

Too late. Heavy footsteps on the stairs and then his door was smashed open. This time there wasn't even some kind of *reason* offered before he was bodyslammed into the wall, posters of Manchester United ripping and sliding behind his shoulder blades; one of the drawing pins rolling and piercing his back.

Fists swung. He dodged some; caught others across his face and head. He tried to shove the rain and whisky soaked attacker away from him but, drunk as he was, the man still had the better grip and double the weight. He seemed to mean serious business this time.

The boy bit down on his hand, drawing blood and a murderous roar of pain. And then made a decision. He was going to disappear. Right now.

1

Three seconds later the man released his grip, his bloodshot eyes wide with disbelief. Spinning around, mouthing wordlessly at the gleaming blue sky, he grabbed at his chest, staggered, and rolled down a sand dune.

1

'Waddayareckon?' asked Jacob.

Alex put a toe into the clear water and abruptly pulled it out again. 'Cold!' he shivered.

Jacob grimaced. It looked inviting in the sun, but he knew their favourite pool was fed by streams from high up in the fells. Even in summer it was not going to be warm.

'Come on!' Alex was already stripping down to blue trunks and goosebumps.

'Mmmmm. Not sure.' Jacob eyed the grassy bank and thought about sunbathing instead. He had his iPod with him. Lazing was looking like a better option.

'Come *on*! It was your idea!' Alex, pulling goggles over his eyes, stepped in up to his knees and let out a little song of shock. 'D-don't wimp out on me!' The goosebumps were mountainous now.

Jacob grinned and shook his head. 'Nah—it'll be more fun lounging on the bank, listening to your whimpers.'

'Death or glory!' yelled Alex, and plunged in head first. He went right under, with an upward flip of his feet, like a dolphin's tail. Alex's shout, as his whole body was submerged, was loud in Jacob's head, but not his ears. His brother couldn't *actually* shout with his face underwater.

So—how is it down there? Jacob asked, grinning as he settled on the bank, his palms behind his head. *Bracing?*

Like a Slush Puppy, Alex gurgled back. *Freeeeezing. You should come in! Ooooh—trout! Just saw a trout! Come IN!*

In a while, sent back his brother, putting his earbuds in and spooling through his album selection screen.

Another trout . . . and . . . tench, I think, went on Alex. He surfaced briefly, took a gasp of air and ducked down again. The pool was smaller than the lake up beside Fenton Lodge. Other kids from the college came down here sometimes, but not often. Usually Jacob and Alex had it to themselves. They had a perfectly good indoor swimming pool too, and they used it a lot, but the pool down here was special. They felt it was *theirs*.

More trout . . . sent Alex.

Jacob sighed. Sometimes the gift of telepathy could be irritating. *OK—enough of the underwater commentary now,* he sent back, *unless you spot a shark! Or a portal to another dimension . . .* He settled back to listen to 'Sir Duke', happily playing air bass-guitar along with it, with his eyes closed.

Look, said Alex, his head bobbing up and then going back under halfway across the pool, *if I can't tell you about my new fishy friends, can you stop channelling Stevie Wonder? It doesn't work in my underwater world . . .*

Jacob turned down the volume on their telepathic link. He could not explain how this was possible—nor could Alex. They'd both been *asked* to explain this, and many other aspects of their Cola talent for telepathy, by the scientists who ran the Development sessions. All kinds of tests had measured the scope of their talent, establishing that while their brother-to-brother link was easy and instinctive; connecting telepathically with others was trickier. Harder work.

Some people were easy to communicate with—

like Lisa and most of the psychic mediums. Assuming they *wanted* to be communicated with. Those with similar talents had learned some time ago how to block other telepaths. Dax Jones, the only Cola who could shapeshift, was also able to pick up their communications, but sometimes not the detail—his form of telepathy was like an animal's. After all, he *was* part-time animal. Top telepaths like Lisa could reach him quite easily, but even she usually needed to make some kind of contact first.

Jacob and Alex had found, though, that even ordinary people could be communicated with on some level, once you'd made eye contact or grabbed their hand or something. They didn't realize it, of course—and they rarely got the detail—but you could definitely plant ideas in their heads. He and Alex were always planting the idea with the kitchen staff that they should get extra cake or biscuits. Mrs Polgammon, head of catering, had only recently worked out what they were doing. Probably one of the teachers had tipped her off.

At the far end of the pool now, Alex rose, flipped over onto his back, and floated lazily under the warmth of the sun. Now that he'd adjusted to the cold water he felt fantastic—invigorated. But he didn't bother to convince his brother to join him. Jacob was lost in his music now.

Alex let the cool water lap into his ears as he floated, submerged to his temples. Occasionally he turned and dipped beneath the surface, where the sun streamed through in shafts of greenish gold, lighting up an amazing world filled with fish and frogs, and then bobbed back up to float on his back again. It was nearly 4 p.m. The day's lessons were over and tea was only an hour away. He flapped his feet, propelling himself along gently. *Good times*, he thought.

Jacob had reached one of his favourite tracks. He turned it up super loud and closed his eyes again to concentrate.

The explosion, when it came, nearly passed him by.

Alex could not believe what he was witnessing. A huge fountain of water was hurling itself up and out, its shock waves rocking him violently in the pool. And something was emerging out of it— shooting back up with as much velocity as it had entered the water. Sparkling droplets flew in every direction, glinting like diamonds in the sun, as a head and two hands erupted from the lake. The eyes were dark, wide and shocked—and one of the hands reached out and grabbed his foot.

'HOME!' gasped the face.

And Alex felt the lake remove itself from his life.

2

Lisa Hardman was perched on the edge of the sofa in the common room, curling a lock of blonde hair around her fingers and peering over Mia's shoulder at a magazine, when the cry sliced through her mind like a blade.

ALEX! ALEX! HE'S GONE! LISA—I NEED DAX! I NEED HIM NOW!

Lisa ran. She would never normally make an effort for a telepath who started shouting in her head so abruptly, but she could feel the panic. Something was badly wrong. Something in the water.

Dax and Gideon were in the tree house at the edge of the small wood. Lisa yelled for Dax and as soon as he'd peered out between the thick green leaves, looking puzzled, she sent him the message

9

direct from her mind. *Get down to the small lake—now! Something's happened to Alex. Jacob's freaking out!*

Dax leapt from the tree house, shifting to a peregrine falcon in mid-air. He shot away through a gap in the trees and arrived at the lake in seconds. Jacob was in the middle of it, taking a lungful of air before submerging himself. In the few seconds that Dax saw the boy's face, his dark brown hair plastered like seaweed across chalky white skin, he knew Lisa was right. Jacob was frantic about his brother. Dax shifted to an otter and dived in, moving fluidly through the water, looking left and right with sharp animal vision. It was stirred up and silty, as if something violent had happened here.

Jacob suddenly bloomed into view, his hair waving in the dim water, staring through goggles at the otter. *Dax! I can't find him! Something's happened to him! Oh god!* he sent.

Employing all his sharp senses, Dax swam a circuit of the small lake, which was no more than a couple of metres deep, and realized that whatever had happened to Alex, he hadn't drowned. He surfaced and leapt gracefully onto the bank where Jacob was slumped, staring across the water, his face grey and frozen. Dax shook water out of his fur, shifted back to boy shape, his jeans and T-shirt dripping, and sat beside him. 'He's not in the lake,' he said.

Jacob pulled off his goggles, shaking his head slowly. 'I know,' he murmured. 'He's not here at all. He's gone.'

'What do you mean, gone?' Dax briskly shook his head, sending another spray of droplets off his thick dark hair. 'Gone where?'

'That's what I'm trying to work out,' gulped Jacob. 'One minute he was swimming around in the lake and the next . . . he was gone.'

'Did he call out?' asked Lisa, arriving next to them, with Gideon puffing close behind.

'No—except . . .' Jacob closed his silver-blue eyes and tried to focus. '. . . just before . . . I wasn't paying attention because I was listening to my iPod . . . but just before he went, he saw something weird—something that made him amazed.'

'Amazed?' repeated Dax, raising his eyebrows.

'Yeah. I can't explain it. I opened my eyes and there were all these big circular ripples on the surface, like there'd been a huge splash. I thought he was messing around . . . but then he didn't come up and he didn't answer me . . . so I dived in and went to find him but . . . *nothing*. He's just . . . gone.'

11

Lisa sat down next to him, touched his shoulder and closed her eyes.

Can you get anything? he sent, instinctively using the open channel she'd offered. *Where is he?*

Hold your horses! I've only just started! she snapped back in his head. Beyond their conversation, Gideon and Dax stood back, watching.

'How can he have just *gone*?' muttered Gideon to Dax. 'He can't have. He's just larking around, I bet. And anyway, he's got tracker chips on him, hasn't he? So the suits up at the lodge will know exactly where he is.'

Dax pointed to the pile of clothes by the bank. 'Do you think they chipped his swimming trunks?' he asked.

Gideon rubbed his tufty fair hair and frowned. 'Wouldn't put it past 'em,' he said. 'We should go and tell them—shouldn't we?'

Dax nodded slowly. He was worried. He liked the Teller brothers. Everyone did . . . with the possible exception of Spook Williams. They were very funny. Aside from their telepathic talent, they had the most entertaining ability of all the Colas. They were gifted mimics and could copy *any* voice with total accuracy. They were a two-brother entertainment

12

unit for the whole college. He'd been doubled up laughing at their antics more times than he could count. One brother without the other seemed very odd. Where *was* Alex?

'I'll just check from above,' he said. He shifted to the falcon and shot high into the air. He coasted around the acres of grounds which surrounded their home, effortlessly riding the warm summer thermals. Fenton Lodge was hidden away in the remotest corner of the Lake District, its extensive grounds surrounded by high, secure walls and guarded by state-of-the-art security—and state-of-the-art military personnel. There was no way Alex could have got out. He couldn't climb the walls—they were electrified along the top. He couldn't dig under them—the barriers continued down into the soil for three metres. And anyway—why would he? He and Jacob loved it here.

There was no sign of the boy below. Dax's falcon eyesight could pick up a mouse in the grass—a teenage boy was no problem. He would have recognized Alex's floppy nut-brown hair in less than a second. There was the small wood, of course, where their tree house was built, which he couldn't see right into. He could do a fox trot through that and use his nose—but now Lisa was talking to them all down by the water, so he flipped over into a stoop and plummeted back down through the warm afternoon air to join them.

'He's not dead,' Lisa said, releasing Jacob's shoulder and getting up.

Jacob stood too, some of the colour beginning to return to his face. 'You're sure? Because . . . I'm not getting *anything*.'

'He's definitely not dead—Sylv has told me,' Lisa reassured him.

'Sylv?' muttered Jacob, wrinkling his brow.

'My spirit guide!'

'Oh—yeah.'

'But he's not here, either. Not anywhere around here,' she said.

'So where has he *gone*?' Jacob raised his palms, exasperated. 'Where?!'

Lisa looked uneasy. 'I really don't know. I can't get a fix on him. I can only be certain of one thing . . . and it's the weirdest thing.'

'What?' demanded Jacob.

Lisa looked around them all. She blew out her cheeks and shook her head, raising her eyebrows. 'He's not in this country.'

3

Alex was hot. Like he was in a steam room or something. He rolled over and felt damp, waxy leaves beneath his bare skin. Where *was* he? He sat up, ripping off his goggles, blinking and trying to focus as a huge wave of nausea swept over him. Everything seemed very green. He must be down by the lake still. Had a storm rolled in? A hot, humid, yet-to-be-broken storm?

But as his eyes at last focused his belly tightened with fear. He was beside a lake—yes—but it was *not* the lake he had dived into. It was very different. The lake which lay a couple of metres away from him was emerald green, reflecting the rich tropical canopy, festooned with heavy, sweet-smelling blossoms, which hung above it. This pool was not much bigger than the small lake at Fenton

15

Lodge, but deeper, by the look of it, with a delicate waterfall plunging into it from a mossy, fern-lined ledge, three or four metres up a craggy slope. It was breathtaking—and Alex's breath was definitely taken. Mostly because he had no clue where he was or how he'd got here.

Panic began to surge up through his chest and lunch began to surge up towards his throat—but he ordered both back down. *No. Stop it. Think! What do you remember?*

He closed his eyes, taking long, slow breaths. He'd been in the lake, floating on his back, staring up into the cloudless sky, while Jacob had been on the bank, listening to his iPod. Then—a tremendous splash and something shooting out of the water and grabbing his ankle.

And then . . . this.

He checked his ankle. It looked normal. He took a few steps towards the pool and sat on a moss-covered boulder at the water's edge. The nausea was easing off now, but he was still on the verge of a major freak out.

Jacob! Are you here too? he sent. Nothing came back. That was alarming. As were the rustles in the greenery and the odd insect-y noises; the peculiar bird calls. Alex got to his feet, turning slowly and taking in his surroundings. There was no sign of any human life here—and no sound of it either. He couldn't hear traffic—no distant road noise, no aeroplanes passing overhead, no human steps through the undergrowth. Nothing. A brilliant flash of red flitted between the trees and he realized it was a parrot. A *parrot*? Where the *hell* was he?

Again he sent out a call to his brother. Again, nothing came back. He simply could not bend his brain around this situation. He must have hit his head on a rock or something, and even now was probably in the medical room with Janey, the college doctor, being nursed back to consciousness by Mia or one of the other healers. This was just a dream.

But if so—how could he *feel* the humid heat? How could his bare feet register the carpet-like touch of the moss on this rock? He pinched himself. Hard. It hurt. Well, if this was a dream, it was the most convincing one he'd ever had. His heart began to thunder inside his chest again. Suppose he never got back? Suppose this was where he stayed for ever, alone in the wild, until he died of starvation or some jungle sickness or a snake bite or something?

'Stop it!' he said, aloud this time so he could hear his voice in this strange place, and convince himself. 'This is freaky . . . but you're not in immediate danger. This is . . .' he gulped, staring around, '. . . an adventure. Just like you've always wanted.'

He waited to feel better. 'HEY!' he called out, suddenly, causing some parrots to flap agitatedly in a tree across the pool. 'ANYONE HERE? ANYONE?'

He held his breath for a response. Nothing.

OK. Get moving. Explore. He badly wished he was wearing more than swimming trunks. Exploring in proper walking boots and shorts and T-shirt would have been so much better. But there was nothing else for it. He took a deep breath and stood up, eyeing the far side of the pool where the water seemed to be flowing out in a stream. If he intended to travel through this jungle or rainforest or whatever it was, he would need a route. You had to follow a river or stream, didn't you? Then at least you knew you were not just wandering aimlessly . . .

He stepped around the boulders, sending some jewel-bright lizards scurrying for cover, and began to pick his way around the edge of the pool. It was tempting simply to swim right across it to where the water streamed across the far ledge—it looked absolutely beautiful. But there could be alligators in it for all he knew. Or piranhas. It smelt beautiful too; a rich mineral scent mixing with the perfume from the brilliant pink and orange blossoms hanging overhead. Strange insects foraged among them, buzzing and chirruping. In less freaky circumstances, Alex would have been fascinated and delighted to study them, but right now he badly needed some sense of purpose and following the stream was the only thing he could think of.

Then there was a crack in the undergrowth. He froze, his heart picking up speed again. He was being watched; he was certain of it. Despite the heat, his skin prickled as he turned slowly around. 'Hello?' he called out. 'Who's there?' He held his breath. Silence. Even the parrots and insects seemed to have shut up. He sighed and turned back to his path—and nearly screamed.

Standing right in front of him was a boy.

The boy looked about his age and size, with dark brown skin and darker brown eyes. His black hair was pulled into tight braided ridges, forming a pattern like a ploughed field across his scalp. He was wearing faded denim cut-off shorts, a white T-shirt, and scuffed trainers on his feet; no socks. All this detail entered Alex's eyes in a second, as he struggled to get control of his shocked breathing. He thumped at his chest. 'Blimey—you scared me nearly to death!' he spluttered. 'Where did you come from?'

The boy didn't speak. He just stared.

'I said . . . where did you come from?' Alex spoke slowly, wondering what language they spoke around here. French? Greek? Swahili?

The boy narrowed his eyes and tilted his head appraisingly. Alex couldn't be sure what was going on—it was hard to read this stranger while he was still so disorientated. The boy's hands were shoved in his pockets and his shoulders were relaxed, but he could be about to pull out a gun or a knife for all Alex knew. He wondered whether his martial arts lessons would be any help when it came to it . . . 'Look—me—' he pointed to his bare chest 'ALEX.' He nodded and smiled and then pointed to the boy's chest. 'You?' he queried.

The boy just went on looking him up and down.

'Oh great!' snapped Alex, rubbing his hands though his damp hair and screwing up his eyes.

'Here I am, stuck in the middle of tropical nowhere, don't know how I got here, don't know how I'm getting out—and the gods and goddesses of Let's Mess With Alex World decide to send me a little helper. Who doesn't speak. Well, just *great*. Thanks a bunch.'

The boy tilted his head the other way this time and bit his lip.

'Cool hair though,' admitted Alex.

'Thanks,' said the boy. 'It took ages.'

They had to swim around the pool before Alex could find out anything else. The boy simply wouldn't tell him until he'd swum. 'It's too hot,' he said, as Alex babbled question after question. *'Who are you? Where are we? How did I get here? What's going on?'* were simply brushed aside. 'Swim first,' he said. 'Cool down. Then we'll speak.' And he dived into the pool, disappearing in a plume of bubbles.

Alex put aside his fears of alligators and piranhas. This boy seemed to think it was safe. Alex dived in after him. He did not want to lose sight of the only human being around. It was a very different experience to the first dip he'd had

21

that day. The water was warm—but still cooler than the air above it. It was silky and fabulous against his skin and even though his heart clattered on with excitement and confusion, he felt soothed. He could see the dark limbs and the white T-shirt of the boy as he darted around in the water. It was clear, despite the green hue, and flowing across a bed of green-grey rocks, continually stirred by the waterfall. Like the pool at the lodge, fish darted in front of him. Unlike the pool at the lodge, brilliantly coloured freshwater crabs moved steadily along the rocky bed.

The boy surfaced under the waterfall, shouting with delight as it spattered across his head and shoulders, pummelling him. He waved to Alex to join him and soon they were both laughing under the fierce massage of the falling stream.

Eventually they swam across to a flat shelf of rock at the edge of the pool and hauled themselves up onto it. Alex had never known a swim quite like this. He would remember it for ever—even if this *did* turn out to be a feverish dream in the midst of a coma.

'OK—let's start again,' puffed Alex, holding out his hand. 'My name's Alex. And yours is . . . ?'

'Olu.' He grabbed Alex's hand. 'Pleased to meet you.'

'I *thought* so!' exclaimed Alex. 'You're English!'

'Well done,' said Olu. 'Manchester born and bred.'

'So what are you doing *here*? Wherever here is?'

'Here is Dominica,' said Olu. 'Jewel of the Caribbean. And I'm here for a swim.'

'Right . . . so . . . here's the thing,' said Alex, staring at him intently. 'Have you any idea what *I'm* doing here?'

'Um . . . kind of,' said Olu. He wrapped his arms around his knees and looked rather awkward.

'Well?!' prodded Alex. 'Because . . . I haven't got a clue. The last thing *I* knew, I was in England.'

'Well, it's sort of my fault,' said Olu. He grinned at Alex, showing a wide set of white teeth. 'Sorry.'

'Sorry? Why?' Alex was beginning to get exasperated.

'I brought you here.'

Alex paused, all kinds of mad scenarios hurrying through his head. This boy had coshed him and kidnapped him and swept him away in a helicopter? Somehow avoiding the military cordon and the state-of-the-art surveillance set up all around the lodge for a ten-kilometre radius? 'HOW did you bring me here? Look—this isn't Alton Towers is it? You haven't just driven me up the road to a Caribbean theme park, have you? This is far, far away from England? This really *is* Dominica?'

'Yep—it is,' agreed Olu. 'It's my chill-out place. I brought you along by mistake.'

'Again . . . *how*?'

'You'll never believe me,' said Olu, with a shrug.

Alex raised his eyebrows and fixed his eyes on Olu's. 'Yeah—well, there are things about *me* you'd never believe too. So try me.'

'It's hard to explain,' said Olu.

'Make an effort!'

'Nah—it's easier to show you. Eat this first.' And he reached around the shelf of rock, away from the water, and pulled out a plastic tub. Alex blinked in astonishment—it was so out of place in this exotic setting. Olu prised open the lid and pulled out a packet of biscuits. A small pack of three Bourbons with chocolate cream filling, like the kind sold in cafes. Alex shook his head. This could not get any weirder. It *had* to be a dream. 'Go on—eat them, or you'll feel really sick afterwards,' said Olu. He ripped open the plastic wrapper and took one, waving the other two at Alex. 'Eat 'em,' he mumbled, through his munching. 'Trust me.'

Alex ate them. They tasted good—intensely real, if this was a dream. He realized that he probably hadn't eaten for a long time. How long had he been here?

'All done?' said Olu.

Alex nodded.

'OK—so, I'll show you how I got you here. Just don't freak out.'

'Go *on*,' urged Alex. 'Get on with it.'

Olu grabbed his wrist. 'Here goes nothing,' he said, and the emerald green pool—the waterfall, the parrots, the blossoms and the insects—disappeared.

4

'You're wasting your time. He's not here,' said Jacob. He'd said it around fifty times now, but still the place was crawling with highly trained military operatives, combing the grounds and lodge and communicating via two-way radios or their wireless earpieces.

Sitting on the bottom step of the grand sweeping staircase in Fenton Lodge's large reception hall, Jacob shook his head, trying to make sense of the last two hours since Alex had vanished. He no longer felt panicky and sick; just incredibly confused. If even Lisa, Cola Club's most talented dowser, could not work out where his brother was, what hope had the people from Control?

David Chambers, head of the Cola Project, stood in the high open doorway, the early evening sun throwing him into a silhouette. His bookish face, with its rimless glasses, was at odds with the close-cropped dark hair and athletic build. It was well known that Chambers had been a soldier in the past. Although he'd run the Cola Project for many years, Jacob could see he'd never quite lost his military edge. 'OK, Jacob. What do you know?' His voice was steady; unemotional. Did Chambers think he was hiding something?

'I've told everyone over and over again,' said Jacob, in a monotone. 'One minute he was in the lake and the next—gone.'

'And you heard nothing—with your ears *or* with your mind?' pressed Chambers.

'Nothing unusual,' said Jacob. He stared at his nails. Two of them were bitten down to the quick. He hadn't bitten his nails for *years*. 'I mean—we're in and out of each other's head all the time. You get used to it. He burbles.'

'He *what*?' Chambers sat down next to Jacob on the step.

'Burbles,' repeated Jacob. 'He's always burbling about something or the other, in my head. And he says I burble too—although it's more musical burbling with me. I was listening to music when he went. He'd asked me to turn it down.'

'He could hear your music?' asked Chambers, furrowing his brow.

'Not through his ears—in my head. In his head. Same thing. He asked me to turn it down—so I turned it down. That means I sort of tune out from him and he tunes out from me. So, if he did say anything just before he went . . . I might have missed it.'

'OK,' Chambers nodded. He got up.

'What are you going to do?' asked Jacob, standing up next to him.

'Search,' said Chambers. 'Use all the government might we have here and abroad—if that's where he is. It's possible he's out of the UK if he was picked up by helicopter. Although *how* a helicopter could get into our airspace undetected I have no idea. We'll use all our available Cola talent too, of course. Principal Sartre is in session with all our dowsers now. They'll find him.'

'No tracker chip showing up anywhere then?' asked Jacob.

'Not so far,' said Chambers. 'There was one in his swimming trunks—yes,' he added, taking in Jacob's incredulous expression, 'even swimming trunks. And now you know why. But we're not picking up anything. The trackers we use are the best available, but nothing is foolproof, as you know.' He turned and rested a palm on Jacob's shoulder. 'We *will* find him. I'm sure of it. Try not to worry.'

Jacob gave him a look. Chambers nodded. 'I know. Stupid thing to say.' He walked away.

Jacob could stand it no longer. He hurried down to Development 4 where Lisa and all the other dowsers were being led by Paulina Sartre. The principal was a powerful dowser herself, but had been outstripped by Lisa a couple of years ago. Lisa was phenomenal at finding lost things or lost people. There were fourteen other dowsers in the college. Many of these types had a mix of ability—some, like Lisa, were psychic or mediums as well as dowsers. Lisa was all three, and way ahead of all the others in her powers. Some of the others were jealous of her, but a handful were wise enough not to be. Lisa's 'gifts' came at a very high price. The spirit world was forever invading her life, despite all her best efforts to discourage it.

Now though, as he pushed open the door to Development 4 and saw them all grouped around a candle, holding hands, eyes closed,

Jacob desperately hoped Lisa would let anyone in. Anyone or anything, from any dimension, who might explain what had happened to his brother.

'Come in, Jacob,' said Paulina Sartre, without even opening her eyes. 'Join the circle—it will help.'

Jacob eased in beside Jessica Moorland and Rachel Price and awkwardly took their hands in his. He was telepathic but he was not like them. He didn't get messages from the spirit world—and was pretty glad about it. He was not on the scale of someone like Lisa, or even Jessica—who'd only recently graduated from telepathy to mediumship. His telepathy was seamless with *Alex*, but harder work with other people, so he didn't really use it that much. He and Alex both felt their biggest Cola power was their mimicry. No other Cola shared their talent for this.

Jacob flexed his lazy telepathy harder, but he wasn't picking up much from the group. A lot of humming mostly. He called to Alex again but got nothing back. Every unanswered call brought him lower.

'Does anyone have anything at all?' asked the principal, her French accent soft in the dim room. 'Anything.'

There was a long silence. Everyone opened their eyes and glanced around at each other, shrugging.

'Something,' said Lisa. 'But it could just be coming from Jacob.'

'What?!' demanded Jacob.

'Bourbon biscuits,' said Lisa.

'Bourbon biscuits?' repeated Jacob, giving her a hard stare.

'I know it sounds stupid,' snapped Lisa, 'but it's what I got. I don't know where he is yet, but he's eating Bourbon biscuits. That should cheer you up. Corpses don't eat biscuits.'

'Come here,' said Jacob, holding out both hands. Lisa glanced at the others. The principal nodded, pushing a stray auburn hair back and smiling a little. Lisa walked around the table and stood in front of him. Jacob took her hands in his and sent *Whatever you got—I don't care how vague—send it to me and me only—NOW!*

Oooh, aren't we masterful all of a sudden? she sent back, tilting her head and raising her eyebrows. But she did as he asked, sending the whole essence of that fleeting contact. Jacob could *smell* chocolate—yes, Bourbon biscuits. And he could feel a sense of great surprise—bafflement. Then

31

sense the satisfaction of consuming those biscuits. He felt flooded with relief. Wherever Alex was . . . he seemed to be OK.

'OK, let me go now, Teller,' said Lisa, cutting into his thoughts. He realized he was still tightly gripping her hands and he let them drop, embarrassed. One or two of the girls giggled.

'Thanks,' he said, looking directly into her dark blue eyes. 'Please . . . keep going. Let me know what you find out.'

Lisa nodded, but it was Jessica Moorland who reached across and squeezed his arm kindly. 'We will,' she said.

The kindness was too much. Jacob got out.

5

The drop in temperature was shocking. It was as if he'd been plunged into a fridge. The warm, moist tropical air evaporated and he was in a world of nothingness . . .

Alex opened his mouth to shout out in alarm, but nothing came from it. There was a roaring sound in his ears, as if he was about to faint, but beyond this, no sound at all. Next, he was smacked down on some unforgiving surface—at which point the tail end of his scream suddenly crashed into his ears at full volume. He grabbed at the ground. It was cold and damp. Opening his eyes he found himself face to face with a carpet of yellowy green lichen. Wind was whipping his hair around and there was a tang of sea salt in the air. Gulls cried overhead.

'How you doin'?' came a cheerful voice off to his left. 'Feeling sick?'

Alex sat up, and once again found his head spinning—but this time it was not so bad. 'I'm OK,' he muttered, gulping as the nausea subsided.

'Good! I told you the biscuits would work, didn't I?' Olu was grinning at him at close quarters. He grabbed his wrist again but this time with his thumb and forefinger, feeling for his pulse. 'Man—that's fast!' he marvelled.

'Where the hell are we?' croaked Alex, gazing around. They were on some kind of headland, the sea in the distance, churning and gunmetal dark. A wide expanse of grey cloud folded low overhead.

'Could be anywhere,' shrugged Olu. 'That's the point.'

Alex, as his head cleared, realized something amazing. 'You teleported us here,' he said.

Olu nodded and grinned some more.

Alex stared at him. 'You're a Cola,' he said.

Olu frowned. 'OK—*amazing*, I was expecting. Incredible. Cosmic and god-like, even . . . but a *fizzy drink*? Didn't see that coming.'

Alex decided to show off. He grinned back and said: 'OK—*amazing*, I was expecting. Incredible.

34

Cosmic and god-like, even . . . but a *fizzy drink*? Didn't see that coming.' It was as if he'd just recorded Olu's words and replayed them across his own tongue.

Olu's jaw fell open and his eyes bulged. 'What did you just do?' he breathed.

Alex laughed. He grasped Olu's shoulder and sent *How about this? Have you ever had anyone chat to you without making use of your ears?*

Olu blinked several times in shock and then backed away, shaking his head. 'You just . . . like . . . got in my head? What the hell are you?'

'Same as you,' said Alex. 'A Cola.'

'A Cola? What the hell does *that* mean?'

'Let me guess,' said Alex. 'You're what—fifteen or sixteen?' Olu nodded. 'Your mum died before you were four.' Olu nodded again, the planes of his face becoming more and more glassy as astonishment took a hold. 'You started noticing that you were—er—*different*—when you were eleven, maybe twelve.'

'How do you know all this?' Olu was shivering. 'Did you just read my mind?'

'Didn't need to. How about you take us somewhere a bit warmer?' suggested Alex. 'And I'll tell you everything I know . . . as long as you tell me everything *you* know.'

Olu nodded slowly and then grabbed Alex's wrist once again. 'Deal,' he said.

This time Alex *was* nearly sick.

'Sorry,' said Olu. 'Three in a row . . . it's not good for the passenger.'

Alex gulped, took several deep breaths, and lay on the carpet, his head spinning. He'd heard that hangovers were like this. He made a mental note to never, ever get drunk. Hey—a carpet! They were indoors somewhere now, at comfortable room temperature—good news for a boy wearing only swimming trunks.

'You OK?' asked Olu, some distance away. 'It's too much—three ports. No more today, OK?'

'There will *have* to be another one,' said Alex, groggily. 'You've got to take me home.'

'No—I can't,' said Olu, firmly. 'Not more than three times in one day.' He walked into a sleek white kitchen and opened a fridge. Alex closed his eyes. It was all too much to take in. Then he felt an icy touch on his arm.

'C'mon! A cola for a Cola!' said Olu, prodding him with the can. There was a *p-shhhh* sound as he flipped the key-tab open.

Alex got up on one elbow and gratefully took the

Coke. He took a long draught and felt the intense sugar hit revive him. He was in a luxurious home—like something out of a magazine. Through one floor-to-ceiling glass wall he could see more tropical greenery. The building clung to the side of a hill and a lush valley fell away beyond a wooden veranda outside. At one end of the open-plan building was some cane furniture, grouped around a glass-topped cane coffee table. The floor was carpeted in some kind of pale, fine-woven wool. An elegant white marble-topped dining table, echoing the kitchen surfaces, was just behind Alex, with six white chairs set around it and a bowl of fresh fruit at its centre. He could hear the soft hum of air conditioning.

'What is this place? Whose is it?' asked Alex.

'Mine,' shrugged Olu.

'Yours?' Alex raised a disbelieving eyebrow. 'Oh come *on!*'

'Well, as good *as*,' said Olu, opening a can of Coke for himself. 'The owners only come out here twice a year. It's a stupid waste. So I live here, apart from the times when they show up.'

'And they don't mind?'

'They don't know.'

'But—that's . . . breaking and entering, isn't it?' Alex shook his head, perplexed.

'Show me any breaking!' laughed Olu. 'I don't need to do that. I just port in here and chill out. And I'm tidy, you know? I don't mess up the joint. I'm like . . . a house-sitter!'

'So . . . are you on your own?' Alex stood and began to wander the room, taking in the large abstract art canvasses on the walls.

'Yup,' said Olu. 'I like it that way. Now . . . what's a Cola? You said you'd tell me.'

Alex paused by the window and stared out at the tropical valley below, still marvelling that he could possibly *be* here only minutes after being on a cold hilltop in god-knows-where. He took another fortifying sip of Coke and began to explain. 'A Cola is a Child Of Limitless Ability. That's the name the British government came up with when they found the first few of us about four years ago. We're all around the same age; none of us have a living blood mother—they all died before any of us reached the age of four. And we all have talents. Unusual talents. Some of us can communicate telepathically, some of us can heal sick people by touching them, some can create illusions or just make themselves disappear, some are telekinetic . . . one can even shapeshift. And one . . .' he turned around to look at Olu, who was leaning on a peninsular unit in the kitchen, staring at him, transfixed, '. . . can teleport.'

Emotions rippled across Olu's face like fast-flowing water—astonishment, excitement, confusion, and concern. 'Only one teleporter?' he asked. 'Who is it? What's his name?' His eyes shone.

Alex chuckled and shook his head. 'His name is Olu,' he said. '*You're* the teleporter. The only one. Welcome to Cola Club.'

Olu's dark eyes glimmered with some emotion that Alex couldn't read. He tried to slip into the boy's head and pick up some clues, but even as the idea came to him Olu put up his hand and said 'Nope. I can feel that. Out you go.' An image of a gate closing flashed back to Alex, and he grinned and nodded with respect. Like most Colas, Olu was a fast learner.

'Olu,' said Alex. 'We've got a lot to talk about.'

'Damn right!' said Olu. 'I mean—what a coincidence! Of all the people to get snagged up on a teleport turnaround—it's *you*. Another kid like *me*!'

'Snagged up?' Alex shook his head. 'How did that happen? You're making it sound accidental—but come on! You accidentally drop into the grounds of Fenton Lodge out of nowhere?! Right into the only place in the world where all the other Colas are?'

'Look—I don't know anything about this Cola club!' said Olu, shaking his head. 'But yeah—it's pretty weird. I'll give you that. We've got a lot to talk about!'

'Yeah—a lot,' went on Alex. 'But look, before we do—is there any chance I could borrow some clothes? I mean . . . it's hard to share when you're half naked . . .'

Olu laughed, throwing back his head and clapping his hands. Alex winced and sat down on one of the cane seats, pulling its satin cushion across his lap. 'I can do better than lend you some of mine,' went on Olu. 'I can get you some cool new stuff.'

And he disappeared. There wasn't even a puff of smoke.

Alex had no idea how long Olu would be gone, so he explored the house. Its three bedrooms, upstairs, had floors of cool, cream coloured stone which stretched into en suite bathrooms with glistening chrome fittings and power showers. The designer furniture was simple and elegant, and there were large original abstract paintings on the walls up here too. In the master bedroom he slid open a glass patio door which led out onto a balcony. Stepping outside was like going into a sauna. He allowed himself to get used to it, though, closing the door behind him to preserve the cool atmosphere inside, so he could drink in the full experience of this exotic valley—the intense perfume of the vegetation; the shrieks of the parakeets which darted between branches of tall trees; the clicks and drones of insects . . . No sound or sign of human neighbours at all, though. He hadn't asked Olu, but he felt sure this was back on Dominica. It smelt the same as the green pool. Olu could obviously go anywhere in the world, but this was the place he had chosen. Alone. Who else was in his life? A father? A foster family? He would ask as soon as the boy reappeared.

The heat sent him back inside. The shocks of the day had left him pretty sweaty and rank, he realized, so he stepped inside a curved glass cubicle and switched on the shower. In seconds, cool water was pummelling his neck and shoulders, gushing out of the large rose above him at high velocity. He gasped, found some shower gel and shampoo on a metal tray in the cubicle, and gave himself a thorough wash, pondering on the wonders of the last few hours. If only Jacob were here to see this! He would LOVE this. Alex decided that the next thing he would ask Olu to do was *not* to take him back to Fenton Lodge . . . but to go back and get Jacob, and bring him here too.

After all, Fenton Lodge might not be such a good idea for Olu, Alex mused. What would Control make of this undiscovered Cola? Was Olu the only one the Cola Project had missed when it began collecting everyone four years back? Maybe there were others around the world that Paulina Sartre had not had enough power to locate through her dowsing talents. But it wasn't this which really occupied his thoughts. It was what the Cola Project might *do* about Olu if he took him back to the college and introduced him. He knew there would be alarm—because how could they possibly keep tabs on a boy like this? It was hard enough for them to hang on to the Colas as it was—especially Dax Jones, who could step right out of his chipped clothes, shapeshift, and fly away if he chose to. In fact, Dax was a celebrated escapee . . . but he had always come back and always managed to justify going AWOL by saving someone's life or something. There was a rumour that his last escape had involved saving the British *Prime Minister*!

So—Olu. A boy who could not be contained. He could be amazingly useful to the project. Every Cola had figured out by now that they would be expected to use their talents for the good of their country. Some of them had issues with it. Some— like Spook Williams—strenuously asserted that they would have their *own* lives, thank you, just as soon as they got to be eighteen and could leave Fenton Lodge. Alex and Jacob had talked about this a lot. They both agreed that any kind of real freedom was unlikely. Colas—especially the telekinetics and illusionists—were just too powerful (and hence too dangerous) to be given the small freedoms that normal people had. And if they *were* let go, how long would it be before they were snatched by another country, desperate to have their powers on tap? So no—it was unlikely that anyone would ever successfully leave Cola Club behind. But Alex didn't want to. Nor did his brother. They loved the college—and he and Jacob both quite fancied being special agents of some kind, fighting terrorists and so on . . . that's why they'd both been training in martial arts for years.

Olu, though, was clearly used to being totally free. And who wouldn't be, if they could go anywhere, anytime—just by blinking or something? How incredible!

But if the scientists at Cola Club ever got their hands on Olu, they would mess with him in all kinds of ways, examine his brain in an MRI scanner, run all kinds of tests . . . measuring his abilities and then trying to work out exactly how they could *stop* them if they chose. They would want control. And they couldn't have it with Olu, could they? So . . . what would they *do*?

Alex switched off the water and stepped out onto the cool tiles, grabbing a thick white towel off a rail and drying himself. His damp trunks lay in a puddle on the floor. He grimaced at the thought of putting them on again and hoped that Olu would come back with underwear too.

He wrapped the towel around his waist and made his way back downstairs. As he reached the living room there was a sudden thud through the atmosphere and he was whacked by displaced air, backside first onto the floor, as a figure suddenly burst out of nowhere.

Olu's face was taut with alarm and he was yelling 'GET OFF!'

And hanging onto Olu was another figure. A man in a uniform was gripping his arm as if it were a buoyancy aid. The man was not young, maybe in his sixties, and his eyes were bulging in his face, while his mouth was opening and closing soundlessly in shock.

'GET OFF ME!' screamed Olu again, finally shaking off his unwelcome passenger.

The man was flung onto the floor where he lay, trying to suck air in and clutching at his chest and throat. Alex stared at the newcomer in complete shock, while Olu angrily threw a large carrier bag across the room and let out a torrent of expletives.

Alex could see the man was in a bad way; his body was going into spasms and he was struggling to breathe. He ran across and bent to touch the stranger's lightly stubbled cheek, watching a blue tinge sweep across it as he did so.

The man's pale grey eyes locked onto Alex's, the question so clearly written in them he had no need to mind read. *How can this BE?*

Alex had no time to explain. A second later the man jerked violently and then laid still, his eyes still open, but no longer seeing.

6

'He's dead,' breathed Alex. His hand was still on the man's cheek and already he could feel the life force was totally gone.

'Bloody fool!' snapped Olu. 'Idiot!'

Alex got up, stepping back from the body in utter dismay. 'What happened? Why did you bring him back with you?'

'I *didn't* bring him back with me!' yelled Olu. He punched one of the heavy seat cushions hard. 'Stupid old fool had to be a hero, didn't he? Had to chase me and grab me—for what? A few quid's worth of clothes and shoes! What did he have to do that for? Eh?'

'So . . . you brought him here by accident, like with me?' asked Alex. Goosebumps were sweeping over him again and he felt sick and

47

light-headed. He had just looked into a man's face right at the moment of his death. The weird *lack* of drama made it almost more shocking. It was so sudden . . . so . . . *over.* He glanced back at the poor security guard—for now he recognized the uniform—and thought about attempting chest compressions or the kiss of life or something. He'd had training, like all the Colas. But he knew it was hopeless. The life force had fled and it was not coming back.

Olu slumped into a chair, looking defeated. 'No—not like you,' he said. 'You're young and fit. You can take it. The old ones . . . the ill ones . . . they can't take it.'

'You mean . . .' Alex took a seat opposite Olu, his knees quite weak, '. . . this has happened before?'

'Yes,' said Olu, not meeting his eyes. 'By accident. I never *mean* it to happen. I didn't mean it to happen *this* time. I ported! To get away from him, but he grabbed me just as I went. I didn't think he had it in him to run that fast—old boy like that. He should have just left it!'

'You were nicking stuff, weren't you?' said Alex. He felt incredibly sad. All this—just because he'd been accidentally ported in his swimming trunks.

'Well—I haven't got a credit card, have I?' snapped Olu. 'I only go to the big stores—where it won't notice. I never nick stuff off *people*.'

Alex picked up the bag full of gear. He was astonished to see the clothes inside it labelled RIVER ISLAND. The price tags were in sterling. 'You went all the way to England for this?' he murmured. Somehow, knowing the dead security guard was English made it worse. He could have been his granddad. He was almost certainly *someone's* granddad.

'England? Japan? Iceland? It's all the same to me,' said Olu. He'd stopped raging now and seemed—incredibly—to be getting over it.

'So . . .' Alex pointed to the body. 'What are we going to do with him?'

Olu sighed and got up. 'I'll take him back. Shop's shut—there's nobody else around.' He walked across and crouched down next to the dead man. 'Sorry, mate,' he said. 'Didn't mean to do you in.' He grasped the man's cooling hand, and both of them disappeared.

Alex stared at the empty space, and then ran to the kitchen sink to be sick.

7

Jacob felt a surge of intense nausea as he sat on the terrace that led out to the grounds to the rear of Fenton Lodge. Gasping, he felt the cool breeze calm him. He knew this wasn't his own sickness, in any case. His insides had been locked down like a sprung trap ever since his brother had vanished.

No, thought Jacob. It was Alex. His little brother, wherever he was in the world, had just upchucked with some violence. The emotion behind it was troubling him most. Alex was shocked and horrified about something. *Alex! What's going on with you?* he sent, desperately hoping this might get through. After all—if *he* was picking up stuff, surely Alex should be able to as well? Their connection had always worked both ways.

Maybe it's only emotions cutting through, he thought. Last time it was surprise, bafflement and wonder and then, oddly, appreciation of chocolate biscuits. So Jacob didn't bother with words this time. He just sent as powerful a punch of his stress and fear as he could. A worried big brother *push*. Would that work?

Jacob let the emotional message fly and then breathed out a long sigh, waiting. After a few seconds he could see Alex in his mind, slumped over, hair flopped across his face, raising a shaky hand to indicate he was OK—he just needed a minute. But that could have been his imagination. A bolt of intense frustration and anger shot through him—and that was *all* his own. He jumped up and marched away to the long, low buildings behind the main lodge, where the scientists and the senior military were based. Chambers had an office here in this modern complex. It was time to find out exactly what Chambers was *doing* about finding Alex. From where Jacob was standing it look like a whole hell of a lot of *nothing*.

Chambers's secretary, a thin young man who took his job extremely seriously, stood up as Jacob strode into the lobby of Chambers's office.

'You know you can't come in here,' he stated, tugging his grey suit jacket sharply across his chest and checking his striped tie. 'Not without an appointment.'

Jacob eyed the man with distaste. *Officious little pen pusher.* He quickly checked the secretary's uppermost mind and discovered that he wasn't *just* being officious; he was afraid.

'Yeah—you *should* be afraid,' he warned.

'Don't . . . *do* that,' said the secretary, urgently reaching under his desk. Now he shuttered his thoughts (all Cola Project staff got some basic training in this) but his fear was very easy to pick up. You didn't need any special power for that.

'Look—I'm not here to freak you out,' snapped Jacob. 'I just need to see Chambers. And you're not going to stop me.' He strode past the desk, ignoring the man's frantic palpations of the emergency button.

'I said—you can't,' insisted the secretary, but Jacob thumped on the smooth, pale oak door anyway. It didn't give. 'CHAMBERS!' he yelled. 'What are you doing to find my brother?!'

There was a buzz and an electronic click, and the door swung inward on his next thump.

'No need to wreck my door,' said Chambers, mildly. He was sitting in a large leather chair, pushed away from his desk, which was covered in books, papers, gadgets, and a small heap of magnetic spheres hanging together in a hand-crafted sculpture above a black plinth. *Magnetite*, Jacob remembered, randomly, from a recent science lesson. *Most magnetic mineral on the planet.* Chambers had his feet up on the desk next to it and a cup of coffee cradled in his hands. He'd been staring out of the tall arched window which gave on to a landscape of green slopes and elegant cedar trees.

'I can't stand this!' said Jacob, suddenly in the middle of the room, the door closing behind him. 'What the hell are you all *doing*? Everyone's carrying on like nothing's happened! But something *has* happened! My brother is gone! Maybe kidnapped! And what are you doing? Nothing! Nothing! Just *sitting* here. And they . . .' he shook his right hand in the vague direction of the lodge's dining room. 'They're all . . .' he could hear his voice cracking, '. . . they're all having *tea*!'

Chambers put down his coffee cup and did something extraordinary.

He stood and walked across to the distressed boy. And gave him a hug.

Jacob let out a series of long, juddering exhalations against Chambers's bizarrely close shoulder, while his eyes blurred and his heartbeat slowly eased. Of all the people at Fenton Lodge, the very last person he would ever have expected to get a hug from was aloof, controlled, enigmatic David Chambers. After a few seconds Chambers led him to a leather sofa on the far side of the window and sat him down. Then he seated himself at the other end and, removing his glasses, rubbed the sockets of his eyes wearily. Jacob noticed, for the first time, that his eyes were a mossy green colour. 'I know,' said Chambers, replacing the glasses. 'You want to punch everyone into a pulp for being so carefree.'

Jacob bit his lip and nodded.

'When I tell you that we are giving this *every* available resource—everything we can think of—' said Chambers, '. . . do you believe me?' He narrowed his eyes a little, gauging Jacob's reaction.

Jacob sighed and nodded. 'Yes,' he whispered. 'It's just . . . I'm his big brother. I'm meant to take care of him. *Why* did I tune him out? Why *then*?

I shouldn't have done that and then I would have *heard* what happened.'

'You tuned him out,' said Chambers, rising, retrieving his coffee, and returning to the end of the sofa, 'because he asked you to. Like he's asked you to a thousand times before. Like you've asked *him* to. You can't *live* in each other's heads—no matter how close you are. It was just bad luck that whatever happened to Alex, happened in that moment when you were disconnected. And maybe it would have made no difference if you *were* connected. We can't know. Not yet, anyway.'

Jacob nodded again, feeling a strange numbness creep over him. He realized he was exhausted. His heart had been pumping in his chest, ready for action, for hours now. The weirdly unexpected hug had finally calmed it.

'When Spook Williams went missing it was the same for Darren—up to a point,' said Chambers. 'And Spook's family, of course. But no matter what emotional rollercoaster they were on, we had to stay focused. That was our best hope of retrieving him. And in the end, we got him back.'

Kind of, thought Jacob. He, along with most of the other telepaths, felt that the Spook who'd come back to them after his ten days missing, earlier that summer, was not quite the Spook who'd been there before. What if Alex came back the same way?

'What are you picking up?' asked Chambers. 'Anything at all?'

Jacob shrugged. 'Nothing helpful. Just emotions. He was sick a short while ago.'

'Do you know why?'

'Because he was shocked about something,' said Jacob. 'But . . . I don't think he's in danger. Lisa said he was eating biscuits before . . .'

'Yes, I heard,' Chambers smiled. 'That sounds very much like Alex when Alex is OK.'

A sudden thought occurred to Jacob. 'Have you told our dad? He'll be freaking out!'

'Not yet,' said Chambers. 'We've been unable to reach him. He's touring Morocco, apparently. In a mobile phone dead zone.'

Jacob nodded. His father was a professional musician and travelling with his band. Simon Teller wrote to them regularly and called at least twice a week. He *should* know about Alex, but Jacob was relieved that, so far, he didn't. The anguish and frustration was awful. He didn't want to wish it on his dad any time soon.

'You need to get some rest,' said Chambers. 'Can I send Mia to you, to help you sleep?'

'I can't be *asleep*!' he argued. 'What if—?'

'Jacob—sleep would be a very good idea,' said Chambers, getting up and guiding him to the door. 'It might be easier for you to pick up a message from Alex when you're in a drowsy state.'

Jacob knew he was right. 'OK,' he said. 'Send Mia.'

When the boy had left, Chambers resumed his position in his desk chair; feet up on the table, cooled coffee cup back in his hand. His eyes rested for a long time on the view outside the window, but he wasn't seeing any of it at all. After a few minutes he placed his cup down on a glass coaster on his desk, got up, and went to a tall oak filing cabinet in the corner. Opening the second drawer down he pulled a file from the hanging folders. It was a thin buff brown folio with only a few papers in it. One word was written on it. *Louisa.*

Chambers pulled a small square photo from the papers. It was a colour shot, but faded with age. He stared at the photo for a long time before slowly closing his eyes, with a deep, slow inhalation, as if, for the past two minutes, he had forgotten to breathe.

8

'You've killed another one?'

Olu nodded, staring into the sun and trying to look impassive. In truth, he felt sick, like he did every time this happened.

Granite laughed and shook his head. 'Oh dear. How many is that now? Six? Seven?'

'It was an accident,' muttered Olu, ripping bits of wiry grass out of the lawn. 'I thought I had time,' he added. 'The old guy was nowhere near me, I swear.'

Granite settled back into his sun lounger, his eyes hidden behind mirror shades and his hair beneath a Panama hat. 'And how is your guest faring?'

'He's fine,' mumbled Olu. 'I'd better get back to him soon, though. He was pretty freaked out by the old boy pegging it in front of him.' Olu couldn't blame Alex. He remembered vividly the first time it had happened to him. Three years ago—and not just some security guard he'd never met before. The first time had been a bit closer to home. The first time . . . it was his dad.

Even though Daryl Stuart had been in the middle of beating his son to a pulp at the time, Olu still felt guilty. It was the first time he'd ever ported with a passenger—and the last time he ever ported his dad. Daryl had lasted five minutes in the Sahara desert. Olu *had* tried to save him, of course, but the man wasn't in great shape to start with—his liver was almost completely shot for a start, thanks to a bottle of whisky a day for as long as Olu could remember. He shivered as he recalled his clumsy attempts at mouth-to-mouth (gagging at the sour taste of cheap alcohol and roll-ups) and then CPR, desperately counting and shoving at his father's ribcage. Eventually, when the pale grey eyes had gone opaque, Olu had sat on the dune in the blistering heat and stared at the body, dumbly, for an hour. When the sand began to drift across his father's blank, stiff face he knew he had to take the body home. Without a body there would be no end of questions and investigations. With a body, the

social services would draw their own conclusions—
that the drink had finally caused a heart attack.

And that's what happened. The pathologist
was puzzled by the sand he found in the corpse's
ears and hair—but not enough to ask any serious
questions. And what could Olu tell anyone? He
gave a version of what had happened as close to the
truth as he could. His broken nose and bleeding
mouth bore witness that he'd been taking another
beating when it happened. Nobody blamed him.
Nobody asked if he and his dad had been on a
different continent at the time of death.

They sent him to a children's home for a short
while, as they tried to search for relatives that might
take him. There were no takers. His mum had had
no family at all, and Daryl Stuart had only a sister
in America with six kids of her own and no desire
for a seventh. The aunt sent him a card with 'In
Sympathy' on it, for the funeral.

So foster parents were found, but Olu never
got to meet them. Instead, he chose to disappear.
Only, unlike so many thousands of abused kids who
were roaming the streets of the UK, Olu really *did*
disappear. He was free—free to reappear wherever
he wanted. It might have taken the death of his

father to make him realize this. It was the one thing he could thank his old man for.

'Have a drink,' said Granite, pushing a tall glass of lemonade across the garden table towards him. 'And don't beat yourself up about it. I know you've never done it deliberately, and most of these people would have been dead soon anyway. You probably did them a favour by making it quick and . . . surprising.'

Olu laughed mirthlessly. 'That's one way of looking at it.'

'You don't have time to wallow,' said Granite. 'You need to get back to Alex Teller and warm him up again—play the sympathy card if need be. Then you need to fetch his brother.'

'I still don't see,' said Olu, 'why it has to be this complicated. Why can't I just port right in and get the guy you really want?'

'Because you'd kill him, dear boy,' said Granite. 'And I don't want that.'

'He's fit! He's a soldier!' said Olu.

'*Was* a soldier,' corrected Granite. 'And undoubtedly still fit. He also has a metal plate in his skull. Port him and you'll both end up covered in his pureed brains.'

Olu grimaced and got up, blocking Granite's sunlight. 'Got it,' he said.

'Come back to me tomorrow,' said Granite, tilting his hat forward as if he was getting ready for a nap. 'When you have the brother. Have a fun sleepover in the meantime.'

'Fun,' said Olu. 'Yeah. I can do fun.' Granite's sunlight flashed back as his visitor vanished.

'How many?' said Alex, when Olu arrived back in the mountain house.

'Hey—looking good,' said Olu, grinning at Alex's clothes. 'I should be a personal shopper.'

Alex was wearing denim cut-off shorts, surfer-style leather beach sandals, and a crushed cotton checked shirt in shades of grey and blue. He looked much more comfortable and assured than he had in just swimming trunks. He was also looking wary and serious, and Olu realized he was trying to get into his head. In fact . . . he'd been in for a good ten seconds, scouting around.

'Seven?' murmured Alex, looking appalled. 'You've killed *seven* people?'

Olu stared at him for a moment. How could he

explain? He shuttered his mind quickly before the boy could rummage through any more of his secrets. 'You don't know what it's like,' he said. 'There's nobody else on this planet like me. How the hell was I to know what would happen if I ported with someone hanging on to me?'

Alex had picked up enough during his sprint through Olu's mind to believe the anguish in the boy's voice. He was convinced Olu had never killed anyone deliberately. But to be so . . . relaxed about it? That was cold.

'OK—you need to know stuff about me,' said Olu. 'And I need to know stuff about you. If we're both in this Coke Club . . .'

'Cola Club,' corrected Alex.

'OK—whatever,' shrugged Olu. 'We need to talk, but I'm starving. Let's eat and talk.'

Alex nodded; amazed that he was getting hungry too, despite all that had happened in the past half an hour.

'What do you fancy?' asked Olu.

Alex sighed and admitted: 'What I really want is some KFC. I haven't had any junk food for *months*. But, hey—whatever you've got in the fridge will do.'

Olu grinned and vanished. Five minutes later

he was back, clutching a red and white cardboard bucket filled with crispy breadcrumb-fried chicken and chips, and a large plastic bottle of Pepsi. Alex groaned with delight as soon as he got the smell.

'Olu,' he said. 'Please tell me . . .'

'. . . that I paid for it?' cut in Olu. 'Yeah! I did! I'm not a total crim, you know.'

'No—tell me . . . that you brought ketchup.'

9

Mia did a good job—as Cola Club's most powerful healer she could calm and console with just a touch of her hand. Like most of the boys here, Jacob was half in love with her, but it was largely due to the 'Mia Effect'—the astonishingly powerful sense of 'feelgood' which emanated from her to anyone close by. At their first meeting Jacob had been besotted, but over time he had grown used to Mia's effect and he, like everyone else, was now able to see her as a friend and act normally.

By just taking his hand for a couple of minutes she had sent him swiftly down through the layers of relaxation until he was calm and drifting into sleep— but as soon as she departed, he was awake again. There had certainly been no time to dream and pick up a message from Alex. He lay staring at the ceiling of their room, the bright sky of the summer evening still sending shafts of pink light through a gap in the curtains at the high mullioned window.

Alex's clothes were lying all over the floor on his side of the room, as if he'd just flung them off and gone to have a shower. There was a Philip Reeve book on his bed—a bookmark in halfway. Normally he would be peering at it by the light of his reading lamp. Where *was* he?

Jacob sent yet another telepathic call, without any real hope of it being answered. After the throwing up business he'd picked up earlier there hadn't been anything else. What if his brother was ill? *Really* ill? The Mia-induced calmness was receding like a tide, exposing ugly rocks of fear and dread. Jacob got up and walked to the window in his pyjama bottoms. He felt hot—feverish almost—as he drew the curtains open and let a slight breeze in through the open window. There was a pulse beating hard in his throat. He gulped and drew a long breath. Maybe he should take a cool shower. He kicked off his pyjama bottoms and was just about to grab his towel from the radiator when there was a sudden thud in the air behind him. It wasn't a noise but a soundless impact which knocked him off his feet.

'Ah good.'

Sprawling on the floor, Jacob looked up to see a strange boy standing by Alex's bed. A black kid with cool hair.

'You're ready to go,' said the boy with a cheerful grin, kicking Jacob's discarded pyjama bottoms to one side. 'We don't want any of them tracker chips coming along with you, do we?'

Before Jacob could say one word the boy leaned across and grabbed his wrist, and the next second there was nothing.

'Here. Drink this.'

Jacob lay face down, shaking. He'd had an inner ear infection when he was ten and it had been the worst thing in the world—the dizziness and disorientation and sickness had been terrifying. This was just as bad.

'Jake! Come on! Drink this; it'll make you feel better.'

Jacob felt his heart lurch with delight. 'Alex!' he yelled, hoarsely, raising himself up on his elbows and looking up.

'Miss me?' beamed his brother, who looked

perfectly well. 'C'mon. Don't want you throwing up on my new clothes.' He pushed a waxed paper cup towards his brother, with a straw in it. Jacob shakily grabbed the straw with his teeth and sucked in the drink—Pepsi if he wasn't mistaken. The ice cold hit of sugar flooded into him fast and he felt the nausea swiftly abate, although he was still shaking.

'Here you go,' said Alex, handing him a robe of light silky material. Jacob abruptly remembered he was stark naked and grabbed it gratefully. Five seconds later he was covered and sitting up.

'What the hell is going on?' he mumbled, trying to take in his surroundings. He seemed to be in a stylish, modernist living room. Somewhere tropical going by the trees and colourful plants outside the tall glass patio doors beside him.

'It's OK—we're fine. We're in Dominica. We're safe,' said Alex. 'And it's really *amazing*. Freaky— but amazing. I've found another Cola.'

As Jacob took in more of the room he noticed a long lost familiar smell. 'Is that . . . *Kentucky Fried Chicken*?' he murmured, amazed.

'Yep! It's still hot! Have some! Have a crispy strip!'

It was the weirdest thing Jacob had ever experienced. He had, apparently, just been teleported, stark naked, from Cumbria to the Caribbean. And now he was being offered KFC. Maybe Mia *had* got him to sleep after all and this was just some insane dream.

There were any number of things he could have said.

What he *did* say was 'Tell me you got some barbecue sauce.'

10

'His name is Olu and he's a teleporter,' said Alex, a few minutes later when they were sitting around the table, helping themselves to hot chips and fried chicken. 'He was just about to tell me all about it over KFC, and then I remembered how much *you* loved this stuff too. So I asked him to go and get you, so we could *both* pig out and hear his story.'

'OK,' said Jacob. He was still in shock and yet somehow managing to shovel in handfuls of chips and crispy fried chicken, dipped in barbecue sauce. More than anything he was flooded with relief. His brother was all right. *Is this guy OK?* he sent. *He hasn't hurt you?*

Hurt me? You're kidding. I could take him any time! sent back Alex. *He's a Cola! The real deal. He didn't even know it until today.*

'OK,' said Alex, aloud. 'Let's start from the beginning. Why did you come and pick me up from our college grounds?'

'Accident,' said Olu, though a mouthful of chips, reaching deep into the bargain bucket and extracting his third chunk of chicken. 'I did a mis-port and nearly ended up splattered.'

'A mis-port?' echoed Alex.

'Yeah,' said Olu. 'Sometimes if I port really fast— like when I'm being chased or something—I have a head problem. I kind of forget where I am and where I'm going. It's like . . . you know . . . hopping in a lift and then forgetting which floor you're meant to be getting out at. Except a lift doesn't usually chuck you out in thin air and send you hurtling towards god knows what at terminal velocity.'

'So . . . you got lost—mid-teleport,' said Alex, taking a slurp of Pepsi.

'Yeah. It doesn't happen often but I was seriously freaking out when I ported and it's like the destinations got mixed up.'

'Why were you freaking out?' asked Alex.

'You won't believe it.'

'Believe what?' prompted Jacob, his sense of unreality easing off as he got caught up in Olu's story and filled his empty belly with fabulous junk food.

'I was about to be eaten by an alligator,' said Olu.

The brothers snorted.

'Told you you wouldn't believe it.' Olu shrugged. 'Doesn't matter. Anyway, believe it or not, I was in the Everglades, slipping like crazy in the mud with this huge, hungry alligator snapping at my legs and I was SO dead—so I ported in a panic. Next thing, I was dropping through thin cloud with no idea where I was going to land. My brain was frozen and all I could think of was that I had to land in water! I thought POOL!'

'Pool? Why pool?' asked Alex.

'Well, that's the weird bit,' said Olu. 'I wanted to go to the green pool, you know, where we first met properly?' Alex nodded. 'I go there all the time, but then I ended up in *your* pool instead! No idea why.'

'So . . . does that mean you can port in randomly to places you've never been?' asked Alex. 'That sounds dangerous.'

'No—I have to have seen it,' said Olu. 'But on telly or in a book or something is good enough. Internet sites—even maps. It has to be in my head. I must have seen your pool somewhere. In a book maybe.'

Alex found it hard to picture this boy flipping through a pictorial guide to the Lake District. He thought Olu's story didn't really add up, but he didn't send this thought to Jacob. Not yet. He wanted his brother to relax and recover from his teleport.

'As soon as I hit the pool and surfaced I realized it was the wrong one,' went on Olu. 'I was a bit panicky, like I said, so I just grabbed for a handhold . . . got your leg or something, and then ported on to the correct pool. I didn't mean to take you with me.'

'Right—so that's how he got here,' said Jacob. 'And then you decided to just 'pop in' and get me. How did you know where to find me? You've never seen inside Fenton Lodge, have you?'

'I just put the picture in his mind,' said Alex. 'I guessed you'd be in our room around now. I couldn't get a message through but I could sense you going off to sleep. And I was right, wasn't I?'

Jacob grinned. 'Were you eating Bourbon biscuits earlier today, by any chance?'

'Yeah—I was—did you get that?' chuckled Alex. 'You know, I *did* keep sending you messages. I knew you'd be worried. I haven't just been larking about, not caring.'

73

'I know,' said Jacob. 'Of course I know. But why couldn't Olu just bring you back?'

'Well—two things,' said Alex. 'One—you *had* to see this place! And two . . . what do you think Control would *do* about him?' He nodded across to Olu who was emptying the last of the fries out of the bucket.

'How do you know he's a Cola?' asked Jacob.

'Dead mother,' said Alex, 'before he was four. Same age as us. Supernatural talent. What else *could* he be?'

'So how come nobody else has found him?' Jacob narrowed his eyes at Olu. The boy seemed likeable, certainly, but he didn't trust him.

'Maybe because he's never in one place long enough. Are you?' asked Alex.

Olu shook his head. 'I got several million air miles,' he grinned.

'Do you port all around the world all the time?' asked Jacob.

'Most days,' said Olu. 'Whenever I fancy it. It's not like it is for you. It's just like stepping into another room. No big deal. I might go to Italy for a nice pizza or Turkey for a kebab . . . sometimes I only stay for thirty seconds,' he shrugged. 'But sometimes I have a lazy day here, just chillin' and playing computer games.'

Jacob took a deep breath just trying to imagine the incredible freedom this Cola enjoyed. It was the absolute opposite of every other Cola's life. To be able to go *anywhere*, at any time, in just the blink of an eye. 'And it doesn't tire you out?' he asked. 'It doesn't make you feel sick or anything?'

'It did to start with,' said Olu. 'When it first happened I thought I was going to die.'

'Tell us,' said Jacob.

'Stop trying to get into my head and I will!' offered Olu, with another grin. 'I can feel it, you know.'

Jacob shrugged and pulled back. He'd not got much anyway—just a lot of images of places Olu had been and one face—a man with pale grey eyes and a pale grey stubbly chin. 'OK—we'll stay out. Tell us how your Cola power arrived . . .'

'And then you can tell me about yours,' added Olu, and the brothers glanced at each other and nodded. *Fair enough*.

'I was bunking off school,' said Olu, chasing one final chip around the bucket with his finger. 'Must've been about eleven, I reckon, because I was just into Year Seven. I was hanging around in this car breaker's yard; looking for stuff . . . you know . . . money dropped out of glove boxes, CDs . . . And gettin' into some of the cars which hadn't been crushed up, yeah? Because some of them are still in really good nick and even the radios work!' He paused—looked at them both and then made a beckoning motion with his hand. 'Ah go on then—come on in and look!'

Jacob and Alex hopped into his mind at once and saw what he was laying out before them—the breaker's yard on a hot sunny afternoon. Lunch time. Workers gone off for lunch somewhere. The smell of old diesel, elderly leather, vinyl and ashtrays. Olu was viewing the yard from the front seat of a BMW—something from the early eighties, looking at the styling, with a steering wheel and a dashboard of matching highly polished wood. The radio was on—a Michael Jackson track. *Billy Jean*, noted Jacob. *Love the bass line on this.*

Alex agreed. *The early stuff's the best.*

'Do you two mind?' asked Olu, aloud. 'Now— pay attention. Here I am, in the car, having a bit of a chill out, but actually it's pretty hot and I've just had a nice sausage roll and some Yop . . .'

Yop—I haven't have Yop for years, sighed Alex, in everyone's head. *They don't do drinking yoghurt at—*

'Look—do you want this story or not?' snapped Olu, suddenly slamming off the visual, leaving only a pale pink emptiness behind.

'Sorry,' said Jacob. 'We'll concentrate. It's good! You're really good at this . . . you must be a bit psychic too.'

'Yeah right—whatever!' grumped Olu, but he opened the vision up again and went on. 'So I'm full up and warm, like, so I go off into a little doze. And then . . .'

Back in the vision there was a tremendous crash and a jolt, and Jacob and Alex juddered violently in their seats. Olu had been rudely awoken by the arrival of four huge claws grinding through the car windows. Shattered glass rained in on him. The world outside the car, still blue-skied and sunny, was swaying about as the BMW was lifted up and hoisted into position above the crusher. Olu screamed, but the breaker's yard equipment screamed louder. He struggled up and began waving out of the newly ventilated rear window space, but the huge metal claws retracted from the roof and the car plummeted into the crusher.

Olu's brain rattled inside his skull as his head connected hard with the roof. His teeth bit through his tongue as his jaw rebounded on impact. Sprawling in the seat, shrieking and tugging the door handles, Olu saw the sunlight depart as the crusher walls and ceiling steadily moved in to grind the BMW into a cube of metal less than a fifth of its current size. Where its passenger's bones, organs and flesh would fit into the puzzle was a question about to be answered by the laws of physics. Olu felt blood fill his mouth from his wounded tongue; he saw the red of it spattering down on the pale blue polo shirt with his school badge on it. He wished, more than anything, that he didn't have to die here. If he had to die, why couldn't it be up on that hill by the Angel of the North? That would be a fitting place to exit the world . . .

And then . . .

'Oh dear god!' Jacob's heart was hammering in his chest. 'You're there. You're *on* the Angel of the North!'

'Yep,' said Olu.

'Remind me . . .' gulped Alex, watching Olu's feet swinging below him as he perched on the huge metal sculpture, '. . . not to get into anyone's near death experience with them again.'

'I thought I *was* dead,' went on Olu. 'That I'd been crushed and killed and I was in some kind of weird heaven . . . you know, *Angel* of the North! And then, maybe I was a ghost.'

Alex grimaced at the long, long drop to the grassy hill. 'OK—I'm coming out,' he said and pulled away from Olu's vision.

'He doesn't do heights.' Jacob explained— but he was pretty shaken up himself. There was no doubting Olu's dramatic story. 'How did you get down?'

'I sat there, shivering, for ages,' said Olu. 'Then I realized that if I was in heaven it was damn cold . . . and my tongue hurt like hell and there was blood all down my front. So it must be real. I had just— somehow—teleported out of the crusher and gone to this place I'd thought of. We'd been there once on a school trip, you see, and I really liked it. And here I was. Up on the top of it, freezing to death. Then I thought . . . *I'd really like to be down by its feet now.* And I was! I thought the dizziness was because I was up high but it was pretty bad even down at the bottom. I threw up all that Yop and sausage roll.

It took quite a few more goes before I got hold of my stomach and stopped all the upchucking.'

'But—didn't anyone see you?' asked Alex. 'Up on the Angel, I mean?'

'Nope,' said Olu. 'Or if they did, they didn't take any photos or video or anything. Nobody was around at all. I had to port one more time to get home before my dad noticed I was late. And then I had to pretend I'd had this fight and got punched in the mouth and . . . anyway . . . that's how it started. Over the next few days I tried it again. Little jumps at first—like, from one room to another. And then I went further—up to Scotland once, to this place my Nan used to take me before she died. It was just like I remembered it; little log cabin by a loch . . . and then I was back in my room, with a big clump of purple Highland heather in my hands. That's when I realized I could take stuff and bring it back too.'

'And nobody knew?' asked Jacob.

'Who was I going to tell?' Olu looked at him like he was an idiot. 'Teleporters Anonymous?'

'OK,' persisted Jacob. 'I get it. But . . . nobody . . . came for you?'

'No,' said Olu. 'Why would they?'

'And you never told your dad?' asked Alex.

The shutters came down immediately in Olu's head and in his eyes. 'Nope,' he said. 'Not my dad. No one.'

'And he still doesn't know?' asked Jacob.

Alex shook his head at his brother. 'No—he's dead, right, Olu?'

'Yep,' said Olu. 'And that's me done. The rest you know . . . I live the teleporter's life now. And it's brilliant. I never want to go back to being normal. I tried that—didn't work.'

'Are you telling me that you've kept it secret for—what—four? Five years?' asked Jacob. 'That *nobody* knows!'

'Yes, I've kept it secret,' said Olu. 'And it wasn't that hard. Even though I've popped up on security cameras and then disappeared, nobody ever takes it seriously. They think it's just a glitch on the tape.' He laughed, throwing back his head. 'You know . . . one Hallowe'en I had *such* a brilliant time on telly!'

'On telly?' echoed Alex.

'Yeah—on one of those shows . . . you know . . . *Spirit Search*, where they go hunting for ghosts in some ruined Victorian asylum or something. I dressed up in an old cotton nightie and started

81

porting all over the place, moaning and drifting about . . .' He began to choke with mirth. 'The film crew nearly wet themselves . . . it was SO funny. Aaaah . . . but it was *wrong*. I only did it once. It was all over the papers, that one!' He wiped away a tear.

Alex and Jacob couldn't help grinning. They would have *loved* to have seen that.

'But anyway—*someone* knows,' added Olu, unexpectedly.

'Oh? Who?' asked Jacob, sitting up straight.

'Can't tell you now, but . . . he kind of looks out for me,' explained Olu with a shrug. 'Just like my dad never did.' Again, Alex saw the grey-eyed, grey-faced man—Olu's dad. He picked up the sweet-'n'-sour scent of old alcohol and fear.

'And . . . I'll take you to meet him tomorrow.'

11

Ryan Proctor stared at the spikes across the screen and, not for the first time, wondered what his client wanted with this clip. To the untrained eye, the image in front of him would resemble the read-out from a seismograph, showing the shocks of an earthquake.

To Ryan, however, it looked like a voice. An unremarkable girl's voice, laid out as an image across his Apple Mac monitor. It had looked a lot messier than this when he'd first received the audio. The sound quality had been pretty poor, with cracks and pops and a lot of tape hiss. He hadn't been able to gate out the hiss completely, but he'd expertly removed the cracks and pops and now the voice could be heard much more clearly.

'It's a lot better,' he told the client, on speaker phone, his voice dampened by the sound-absorbing panels which were hung artfully around his production studio. 'But not perfect.'

'Please play it,' commanded the voice—a cultured English voice with an undertone of something Ryan hadn't yet been able to name. Something which made him shiver.

'OK, here goes,' he said, and threw the fader. A vertical bar immediately began to travel across the spiky pathway on his monitor and a young girl's voice spoke out from his expensive Bose speakers.

Hi Mum . . . going to be a bit late . . . Me and David are going round Emma's for a while and then we're coming back over the park. I'm taking Rusty with me for the walk. Should be back by . . . um . . . five? OK? Seeya . . .

The audio image ended with a big, thick, column which stretched from the top of the screen to the bottom—the resounding click of a phone being hung up. Something about it sounded horribly final to Ryan. He shivered again. The sooner this job was over, the better. And no—he had no desire to meet the owner of that cultured English voice, either. He was very glad he could send the file as an email attachment. He rocked on his leather studio chair, nervous for no reason that he could define.

'Much better,' said the client. 'Thank you, Mr

Proctor. Now . . . what can you do to age that voice by twenty years?'

Ryan stopped rocking. 'You want her to sound twenty years older?'

'I do,' said the client.

'I can do that,' said Ryan. He rattled instructions across the keyboard, conscious of the lengthening silence as the client waited. Then he played it back.

The girl had become a woman.

'Thank you, Mr Proctor,' said the client. 'Thank you very much.'

12

Olu had brought more than one set of clothes back from his 'shopping' spree some hours earlier. Alex was nearly as tall as Jacob and not much skinnier, so the stuff Olu had picked up also worked for Jacob.

'Thanks.' Jacob grabbed a pair of blue jeans and a dark red zip-up sweatshirt. There was a multi-pack of jersey undershorts too, and another pair of canvas deck shoes. 'Where'd you get all this?' he asked. He noticed that Alex was quiet and his eyes were downcast. *What?* he asked, directly into his brother's head.

You don't want to know, sent back Alex.

Maybe not, but you have to tell me anyway . . . it's to do with you throwing up earlier, isn't it?

'You'd better tell him,' said Alex, looking at Olu.

'I can't keep it from him. He's in my head all the time, like I'm in his.'

Olu looked uneasy. Guilty. He'd been stuffing the KFC cartons into a plastic bin bag in the kitchen. 'OK. Look, Jacob—we, um, we had a death earlier today.'

'A death?' Jacob stared from Olu to Alex and back again. They looked serious.

'It happens sometimes,' said Olu.

'Yes—it happens a lot,' said Jacob. 'People die every day—but what do you mean "*we* had a death"? We're not paramedics! Alex?!'

'It wasn't *his* fault,' said Olu, quickly. 'It was nothing to do with him. I ported somebody here by accident . . . and the shock killed him.'

'*Somebody*? Who?' Jacob felt his insides lurch. This was *not* what he wanted to hear from Olu. He had sensed that the boy had stuff to hide . . . but didn't every Cola? Death, though? Accidental or otherwise—a *death*?

'It was when he was getting the clothes,' explained Alex. He sighed and shook his head. 'It was horrible. This old bloke . . . security guard from the shop . . . grabbed hold of him just as he ported back and then . . . had a heart attack or

87

something. It was so *fast*. I tried to help him but . . . he just died.'

Jacob rounded on his brother. 'So . . . bringing me here and eating some KFC—that was your priority after this bloke dies right in front of you?!'

Alex shook his head. 'I wasn't hiding it from you—I just . . . needed to be normal for a little while before I told you. If I'd told you as soon as you got here you would have gone mental.'

Jacob gripped the back of a dining chair and marshalled his breathing. 'But how did you know he wouldn't bring *me* through having a heart attack?' he demanded.

'Oh no—wouldn't happen,' said Olu. 'It's just people with like, you know, health problems. Old people or people with dodgy hearts and stuff. Young, fit guys . . . no problem. I checked with Alex before I went to get you.'

'Would you rather we'd left you at Fenton Lodge?' muttered Alex.

Jacob sighed. 'No . . . no, of course not. It's just . . .' He rubbed his hands over his face, suddenly desperately tired. 'This is such a weird day.' He looked around the room. 'What did you do with the body?'

'Took it back,' said Olu. 'They'll find him in the morning—just think it was an ordinary heart attack, that's all.'

'And this has happened before?' asked Jacob.

'Yes—a few times,' muttered Olu, staring down at his feet. 'But always by accident, yeah? You don't think I do it for a laugh, do you?'

There was no doubting the look on the boy's face or the chilled note in his voice. Jacob shook his head. 'I think you should take us both back now,' he said, his voice low and measured.

'I will,' said Olu. 'After you've had some sleep. *You'd* probably be OK, but I've already ported Alex three times today . . . and that's too much. It wouldn't kill him or anything . . . but it would make him really sick to go again so soon. He's not used to it.'

'What about Dad?' Alex asked, suddenly remembering. 'He'll be freaking out!'

'It's OK,' said Jacob. 'Chambers couldn't get hold of him—he's with the band somewhere in the back of beyond right now. No phone signal.'

'Good,' said Alex, nodding with relief. 'But the others—Lisa and Jessica and all that lot—they'll be dowsing for us too. Will they find us, do you think?'

89

Jacob shrugged. 'Well, even Lisa wasn't getting a fix on you before. I was there when she tried. The only clue she really got was the biscuits thing. Probably because you were porting all over the place. But she might pick us up now—now that we've stayed put here a while and we're both together.'

'Let's just send her a "don't worry" message,' said Alex. 'And then block her off for a few hours. I don't want a load of helicopters suddenly arriving here.' He grabbed his brother's hand, knowing that together they would send a powerful signal, and let Jacob hurl the message out into the ether, somewhere in the direction of Lisa's reluctant psychic aerial. *Lisa—we're OK. We'll be back in the morning. Tell Chambers not to worry. Well . . . don't tell him anything. It'll be fine.*

They waited a few seconds, just in case they got something back, but nothing came.

'Nah—we're too far away,' said Jacob. He turned to look at Olu who was watching them both with awed fascination. 'We'll get some sleep then, and in the morning you take us back, OK?'

'No problem,' said Olu. 'Although I'd like to take you to meet Granite first.'

'Granite?'

'Yeah—the guy who looks out for me. He'd love to meet you two. It wouldn't take five minutes and then I'll port you both back to your college.'

'OK,' agreed Jacob. 'Five minutes to say hello . . . that's all.' His head swam suddenly, and the full weight of exhaustion from his fearful, panicky, amazing day hit him.

'C'mon,' Alex took his arm. 'We've got really a cool bedroom!'

They could have had a room each but chose to stay together in the one which had twin beds. Jacob wandered around it, dumb with exhaustion but still marvelling at the luxury. 'Check out the power shower!' advised Alex. Jacob did, shedding the new clothes and finally getting on with the shower he had first intended to have two hours ago back at Fenton Lodge.

Afterwards he sank into the cool light sheets of the bed across from Alex's. The air conditioning droned quietly. Beyond the double-glazed windows the sky was still bright, bathing the swaying palm trees in gold. They were five hours behind UK time, Olu had told them. They'd be porting home sometime in the middle of the Dominican night.

'What do you think about him, really?' Jacob yawned, and Alex pursed his mouth and stared up at the ceiling.

'He's OK—but he's seen some bad stuff. Even before he got Cola powers, I think. It's made him a bit . . . wonky.'

'Do you think we can trust him?' asked Jacob. 'Because I don't. I like him . . . but I don't trust him.'

'I know what you mean,' said Alex. 'He's hiding stuff—but I don't know if it's anything to do with you and me, or if he's just so used to hiding his talent from people that it's there all the time.'

'We should have worked harder in Development sessions,' sighed Jacob. 'We could have got into his head much better then, without him noticing so quickly. Lisa would know everything there was to know about him in seconds.'

'Yeah—but would she have bothered to look?' grinned Alex. Everyone knew that Lisa didn't do mind reading unless she had to. She really didn't *want* to get inside people's heads. 'I think he's OK. I think he likes us. He's excited to have someone his own age that he can share all this with. Jake— imagine—with a mate like Olu . . . we could go *anywhere*!'

'Yeah? And how long before Control finds us and ships us back home?' asked Jacob.

'No chips on us,' said Alex. 'You came through in the nuddy, and I had only those trunks on. And Olu ported those to Iceland on the way to getting you!' He chuckled, picturing a crack team of special Cola Project operatives storming across the icy tundra in search of their lost asset . . . only to find a pair of frozen swimming trunks dangling off a twig. He shared the image and the joke with Jacob, who had to laugh too.

'Come *on* . . .' said Alex. 'This is an adventure! A real . . . amazing . . . brilliant adventure! Haven't you always wanted something like this? We've got it for a few more hours, whatever happens, so we might as well enjoy it.'

'Fair point,' said Jacob, waves of sleep beginning to steal over him. He settled his head comfortably on the pillow. 'Adventure in the morning. Sleep now. Night . . .'

'Yeah. Good plan,' agreed Alex. 'Good times . . .'

13

Jacob and Alex sat up on the sloping grass, shaking their heads and catching their breath. After a good breakfast of tea and bacon sandwiches, they were handling their latest port well, noted Olu with satisfaction. He helped them to their feet

'OLU!' called Granite, standing. 'Good to see you! Introduce me to your friends.' He ambled across the lawn towards them, looking like a genial uncle in his checked shirt, Panama hat and crumpled linen trousers.

'Granite—meet Jacob and Alex Teller!' called Olu.

'I'm so excited to meet you,' said Granite, grasping first Jacob's and then Alex's hand in a firm shake. 'You are the first friends Olu has ever trusted to share his secret. When he dropped in earlier to tell me, I told him I *had* to meet you. Please—please, sit down.' He waved them over to chairs at a garden table laden with glasses and a tall jug. 'Have some lemonade.'

Jacob and Alex, still battling some queasiness from the latest teleport, drank quickly and began to feel revived. Alex studied Olu's friend with interest, noting the odd, green-tinted glasses, the battered hat, and the silver ring on the middle finger of his left hand with some kind of shiny grey-black rock set into it. At first glance the man seemed old—he looked as if he could be in his sixties—and yet he moved, even sitting down, like a man half that age.

Alex slid his thoughts across to his brother and Jacob took them, barely aware of the process. He was still recovering from the disorientation of his latest teleport and not yet making notes himself. 'Where are we?' he asked, putting his drained glass down.

'I can't tell you precisely, out of concern for Olu,' said Granite, settling into his seat and looking at Olu with a grandfatherly expression on his face. 'But we're on an island some way north of the UK.'

As Jacob gazed around, Alex realized this was the place Olu had ported him to just after the meeting at the green pool. Only this time it was a much warmer day. They were in a large garden on a slope which led down towards a cliff maybe half a kilometre away. He couldn't see the beach below it but could make out—across the low hedge boundaries—blue sea in the distance, a jutting headland of black volcanic rock topped with bright green turf, and a distant settlement; cotton thin smoke trails rising from its chimneys.

'How did you meet Olu?' asked Jacob. He had tried to get into the man's head for a few clues but had found it completely shuttered. Startlingly shuttered.

'Well—it wasn't the best start,' said Granite. 'I killed him.'

There was a stunned pause during which Olu ate a biscuit whole and then guffawed at them all, spraying crumbs across the table. 'It's true,' he laughed. 'Well . . . almost.'

'It *is* true,' confirmed Granite. 'I was driving through Switzerland when Olu decided to teleport in right in front of me. The first I ever saw of him was his backside smashing my windscreen.'

Jacob and Alex stared from the man to Olu and the boy nodded faster, still grinning. 'Really nice car too,' he said. 'Lamborghini. Gallardo Spyder. I wrecked it!'

'Yes,' sighed Granite. 'Many thousands of pounds worth of damage.'

There was a moment of silence as all four acknowledged the pain.

'But Olu came off the worst,' went on Granite. 'Fractured skull, broken pelvis, broken leg, internal bleeding . . . I could go on. He wasn't breathing when I got out of the car—just a crumpled empty dead thing at the side of the road. Fortunately I have some skill at resuscitation and managed to get him breathing again and off to a little clinic I know in the area.'

'I woke up,' continued Olu, 'All straps and bandages and a leg cast and stuff. I didn't know where I was. There were, like, *nuns* looking after me, all speaking French or German. Like *The Sound of Music*! And for the first time I couldn't just port out, because—well, how was I going to treat my own broken bones?'

'I realized Olu was something . . . exceptional,' went on Granite. 'It's not every day a teenager steps into your world from another dimension. I got him to talk to me, found out his name—and

97

that was all, to start with. Then I told him I *knew* what he was. A teleporter. Or a walk-in, as they're sometimes known. And that it was fine by me.'

'I was freaking out,' added Olu. 'Nobody—*nobody* had ever actually said that to me. Nobody knew before. But here was this bloke saying "Hey—it's cool."' Olu's face showed a brief flicker of some emotion; gone as soon as Jacob saw it.

'So . . . I brought him back here when he was better,' said Granite. 'Or rather, he brought *me*—as soon as we'd worked out I was fit enough and he wasn't going to explode my inner workings, that is.' He beamed at them all and nodded reassuringly. 'And, ever since, Olu has been a regular visitor. I like to think we are almost . . . family.'

'Why do you call him Granite?' asked Jacob, suddenly certain that this was not the man's real name.

Olu looked a little more serious. 'Cos he's my rock—you know?'

Alex snorted.

'No—I don't mean it like . . . a Celine Dion song or something,' explained Olu, getting to his feet. 'What I mean is . . . I can't move him. Not unless he wants me to. He knows how to stay put when

I try to port him. And that's really cool. He's the only one I've ever met who can do that.' He stood behind the man, grabbed his shoulders, and then disappeared. Granite, though, stayed put, his hands clasped in his lap, as Olu came back, shrugging. 'See! Can't make him go. Not unless he wants to.'

'So, what's your real name?' asked Jacob.

'I go by lots of names,' said Granite. 'But I want to know about *you* two. Olu tells me you have special powers too. Telepathy? Yes? And mimicry?'

How much can we tell him? Alex sent, immediately.

I don't know, Jacob sent back. *He seems to know a lot already. Let me do the talking for now . . .*

'Yes—we can communicate with each other,' said Jacob, nodding across to Alex. 'But that's about it. We're not really that good at it. With other people it doesn't work so well.'

'Not even with your friends back at Cola Club?' asked Granite.

Jacob and Alex exchanged shocked glances. He *knew*? Just how much had Olu told him?!

'Don't distress yourselves,' said Granite, sitting forward in his chair and fixing them with a serious expression. 'It's all right. I am in the business of knowing secrets, but I am not in the business of giving them away. There is a lot of chatter out in the world about Colas. Of course, many people think it's some twenty-first-century urban legend, but a few of us . . . well, we know different. You're two of about 100 Children Of Limitless Ability who the British government likes to keep cloistered somewhere in Cumbria, yes?'

Jacob and Alex said nothing. Alex felt a surge of annoyance at Olu, that he had brought them to this man without warning them of what he knew. Olu, though, on his fourth biscuit, looked supremely unconcerned.

Jacob felt chilled. Olu's story of 'accidentally' porting Alex was looking more and more feeble. This man—Olu's 'rock'—knew far, far too much.

'Olu,' said Jacob. 'I think it's time you took us back.'

Olu looked surprised and rather hurt. 'What—already?'

Granite sat back in his chair and shook his head sadly. 'I'm sorry, Jacob. I've scared you. I really didn't mean to.'

'You have not *scared* me,' said Jacob, his jaw clenched. He tried again to get into the man's mind, but once again, found only shutters.

'I imagine it was fairly scary when you first met Owen Hind and Paulina Sartre and got taken away by the Cola Project,' went on Granite. 'Just days after the school talent show, I gather. Do you remember?'

'How do you know all this?' said Jacob. 'Who are you really?'

'He's all right, Jake!' said Olu. 'You can trust him! C'mon! You said you were going to tell me your story like I told you mine! Tell us—and then I'll take you back.'

This is really not good, Jacob sent to Alex.

I know, his brother sent back. *I'm sorry I got you into this. I'm really sorry, Jake.*

Don't be, sent back Jacob, *You did the right thing, getting me here. I just don't know if we're going to get back. I'm going to play along a bit. You try to get into this guy's head while he's listening—OK? But don't be obvious . . . he's too smart.*

Jacob had been staring at his lemonade during this exchange. Now he looked up, glanced around them all and shrugged. 'OK—I'll tell you—and then you HAVE to get us back, Olu. Our friends will be going nuts by now.'

'Sure—no problem,' said Olu. 'So . . . tell!'

'Alex was eleven—and I was twelve,' said Jacob. 'We were idiots. We had no idea what we were doing.'

14

At first they'd had a brilliant time. They'd always been good at sending people up—doing their voices and their mannerisms. They used to do a little comedy act in the school talent show every year, taking the mickey out of the teachers, the prefects, the school caretaker—anyone with a good accent or funny quirks. Yeah. They were good. But not setting the world on fire.

The mimicry—the *real* Cola mimicry—came later. First it was the telepathy. It started at a quiz. Jacob was in the same house as Alex, even though they were a year apart at school, and so they both ended up on a house quiz team one day, competing against the three other houses in the school. With Venturers neck and neck in the lead with Aviators, Alex got the subject of Music. Jacob had been hoping to get Music for himself—he was *sure* he'd know all the answers to this category; he lived, breathed and *slept* music.

'What is the name of the Beatles' fourth album?' asked the teacher.

Beatles for Sale! Jacob shouted in his head as Alex screwed up his eyes, trying to remember. Dad had played pretty much every album to them many times, so he might get it right, thought Jacob, but even as this thought crossed his mind he *knew* Alex was going to say '*Help*!' He could even see him draw in the breath and form the aitch.

Nooooo! he sent. *Not* Help! *That's the fifth album. Beatles for Sale . . .*

Alex said, 'He—he-hmmm. *Beatles for Sale?*'

'Correct!' said Mr Riley. 'Well done. Now—what were the first and second names of Mozart?'

'Um . . .' Alex wrinkled his brow again and Jacob clearly heard him mumble *Amadeus? Amadeus something?* and yet his brother had not moved his lips. Jacob looked around at Mr Riley, at the other teachers and the other teams. Nobody seemed to have noticed that his brother had suddenly become a ventriloquist. *Oooh—what's the other name?* anguished Alex, as clearly as if he was right next to

Jacob's ear, and yet there he was, sitting three or four metres away from the team table with his hand firmly over his mouth as he concentrated hard.

Wolfgang, you noob! sent Jacob. *Wolfgang Amadeus Mozart!*

Alex's eyebrows shot up in surprise and he said, 'Wolfgang Amadeus.' This time he *was* using his mouth.

Everyone clapped and the other two Venturers on their team whooped a little but Jacob was silent. He was getting goosebumps. What was going on here?

The next two questions Alex needed no help with. The answers popped into his head easily. Jacob could hear them arriving a second before Alex spoke them. Then came another tricky one.

'Who co-wrote and performed the 1960s classic,' said Mr Riley, '"Sittin' on the Dock of the Bay"?'

Alex was stumped. Nothing came into his head at all. He was just about to say 'Pass' when Jacob shouted, in his mind, *Otis Redding! It's Otis Redding!*

Alex suddenly looked at Jacob in shock. But his brother was sitting silently next to their team mates, looking rather spaced out.

'Um . . . is it . . . Otis Redding?' he asked.

'It *is* Otis Redding! Well *done*, Alex!' Mr Riley was clearly impressed.

Alex barely heard him. Jacob was in his head. Jacob was saying *Is this just me or are you freaking out now too?*

I am most definitely freaking out, sent back Alex. *If you really can hear me, turn around and poke Josh on the ear.*

Jacob grinned, shook his head, and then turned and poked Josh's ear.

'Oy!' squawked Josh.

'Sorry—there was a bug on it,' mumbled Jacob as Alex walked back to the table, still being applauded, but absolutely oblivious.

Anyone looking closely would have noticed that the Teller brothers were abnormally quiet for the rest of the quiz. The Venturers house team won it easily, because Jacob picked up the Natural History round at the end and Alex supplied him with two-thirds of the answers.

On the way home from school, shaking with excitement and not a little fear, they practised again and again, and every time, it worked. They *could* get into each other's heads. They could talk telepathically. It was the coolest thing they could ever possibly have imagined.

Until the mimicry arrived, two days later.

'We were idiots,' Jacob told Olu and Granite, refilling his lemonade glass. His insides felt tense. *Anything?* He sent to Alex and Alex gave a tiny shake of the head. *Can't get in. He knows how to block.* Jacob took a deep breath and pressed on. Telling their story here on this remote island, not knowing for sure where he and Alex would end up next, was not relaxing. And yet it was compelling. Olu and Granite echoed the amazement and excitement he and Alex had felt at the time. 'We didn't know how to keep a lid on it,' Jacob continued. 'We started doing little shows. Mind trick things with the other kids. We couldn't get into *their* heads back then— well, only a little, but I don't think we were aware of it. We just started getting them to draw things on a bit of paper and I would be blindfolded with my head in a bucket or something and Alex would be out in the crowd, watching the picture getting drawn and then he'd just send it right into my head, and I would draw exactly the same thing as soon as my blindfold was off. It was brilliant—the kids were knocked out! We were a sensation.'

'And if you think *that* got people excited . . .' said Alex, finally giving up on probing Granite's mind and joining in, '. . . imagine what happened when the mimicry arrived. I was doing a send-up of Gavin Carpenter, this idiot kid in Year Ten who liked to set fire to his own farts for a laugh. And then . . . it wasn't just a send-up any more. His voice just came out of me. *Exactly the same.* At first I thought he'd sneaked up behind me or something and had just talked across me. But he wasn't anywhere in sight.'

'I got him to do other people we knew,' said Jacob. 'Teachers, Dad, students—people off the telly. He could do *them all.* Exactly. Like a tape recording.'

'Word for word, nuance for nuance?' asked Granite.

'Word for word, nuance for nuance,' confirmed Alex, in an exact facsimile of Granite's query.

Granite took a long breath and his eyes glimmered behind the tinted lenses. 'I see,' he said, rubbing his long fingers across his chin.

'The next day Jacob could do it too,' said Alex. 'Just in time for the end-of-year talent show. We did the most amazing act anyone had ever seen. People reckoned we'd set up some kind of audio system and were lip syncing—that's the only way they could get their heads around it.'

'It was weird,' said Jacob, staring into his glass but seeing the audience that night again. The hilarity . . . the amazement . . . the clapping and cheering . . . and the first arrival of the fear, flickering uncertainly, like a distant forest fire, across the rows of agog faces. 'And first thing the next day this guy called Owen Hind shows up at our house—and we never go back to our school again. Two weeks later we're in Cornwall, at Tregarren College, with another six weirdos who have suddenly freaked people out by doing something amazing and scary. Then more came. Then more, until there were about 100 of us. And that's it. That's how it happened.'

'How did your father cope?' asked Granite, softly.

'He was scared when he realized we really could do the telepathy thing,' said Alex. 'He didn't really show it, but we knew. And when the mimicry thing came out he was angry—he said he couldn't believe we'd been so dumb as to do that show; to let everyone know how . . . different we were. He knew it meant danger for us, sooner or later. It took a long time for Owen Hind to convince him to let us go, but in the end he was all for it, because he could see that we were never going to be able to hide what we could do if we just tried to go on as normal. We needed to learn how to manage it, and that's what Owen Hind promised Dad he'd teach us. And he did.'

'Extraordinary,' said Granite. 'And does anyone else at Cola Club have this talent?'

'No,' said Jacob. 'Loads of them have got telepathy—some just a little bit, some loads. We're average. But we are the only ones who can mimic.'

'Illusionists can be quite good at it,' added Alex, thinking of some of Spook Williams's illusions and how the sound that went with them was usually pretty convincing. 'But if you listen properly they're not really mimicking. Not like we do. Mostly it's visual and everyone's ears kind of invite the audio in and assume it's right.'

You're telling him too much, sent Jacob. *He doesn't need to know all this.*

All right! All right! snapped back Alex. *But I reckon he knows anyway!*

Granite stood up. 'I'd like to try out a couple of things with you, back at the house. Would you mind?'

Jacob and Alex exchanged glances, uncertain.

'Then I'll take you back home,' said Olu. 'Come on!' And he grabbed their arms and a second later they were inside a house.

15

'*Olu!*' Jacob swayed and grabbed for the sill of a tall window. 'You could have warned us!'

'Nah—you're getting used to it,' said Olu. 'You're fit and healthy. You won't even blink next time.'

Jacob realized he was probably right. Alex was looking fine, just shaking his head and gulping, and he himself felt only a little dizzy this time. He took a long slow breath and looked around. They were in a hexagonal room with walls of whitewashed tongue and groove wood, and windows giving out onto a spectacular view of the coast. The floor had a thick chocolate-brown carpet, upon which stood a round dining table with four chairs. On the table's cream cloth sat an expensive looking MP3 dock, torpedo-shaped to accommodate its speakers.

111

'Sit down,' said Olu. 'He'll be here in a minute.'

'Everybody fit and well?' asked Granite, as he stepped into the room. He took off his hat, revealing thick silvery white hair, and joined them at the table, choosing the seat closest to the MP3 dock. 'Good. Now . . . Jacob and Alex. Can you mimic girls? Women?'

'Easily,' said Jacob.

'OK—try this,' said Granite, and he pressed PLAY on the small silver MP3 set into the dock. At once a woman's voice rang out of it.

'Hi Mum . . . going to be a bit late . . .'

Granite hit pause and looked at Jacob. He raised an eyebrow.

Jacob shrugged and repeated 'Hi Mum . . . going to be a bit late . . .' It was perfect—right down to the breathy, slightly guilty pause after 'Hi Mum'.

Granite smiled and nodded to Alex, who uttered precisely the same thing.

'OK—but that's just eight words. How about the rest of it?' Granite pressed play again and the woman spoke on.

'Me and David are going round Emma's for a while and then we're coming back over the park. I'm taking

112

Rusty with me for the walk. Should be back by . . . um . . . five? OK? Seeya . . .'

Again, Jacob and Alex repeated—word, breath, tone and timbre perfect.

'So . . . you're a pair of human tape recorders,' mused Granite, his face a picture of fascination. 'But can you pick up this voice and make it talk about other things—random things—and still hold the voice?'

'With enough to listen to, it's no problem,' said Jacob. 'Might have been hard with just those first eight words. You need to study inflection and accent of course.'

'But you've heard enough of this—er—lady to be able to improvise?' asked Granite.

'Hi Mum,' said Alex, once more riding the woman's voice. 'How are you today? I've just been down the road and bought sausages and I tripped over the cat and broke both my legs! Can you send a vet for the cat, an ambulance for me and some beans for the sausages?'

Olu hooted with laughter and Jacob smiled. Alex had always been the King of Random. Granite was chuckling too, although he was looking very thoughtful and it occurred to Jacob that this little

MP3 set up was awfully 'convenient'. He realized, with a thud in his chest, that this meeting had been planned. Carefully.

'Try this,' said Granite, and hit play again. This time it was the voice of a man. A middle aged man, privileged, upper class, Jacob guessed.

The new voice rang out curtly. 'I don't care what excuses you've come up with today, Harris. I have a half hour window open at 2 p.m. and I expect you to be there. If you can't make it I shall assume you agree to the foreclosure and will instruct my people to proceed. Good day.'

'Nice man!' joked Olu.

'Rich man,' said Granite. 'Corrupt, ruthless . . . and loaded.'

'I don't care what excuses you've come up with today, Harris,' said Alex, with spot-on delivery as usual. 'I'm going to wear the little red dress and the frilly knickers and that's an end to it.'

Olu choked with laughter again and Jacob grinned too, but a feeling of disquiet was descending though him, trickling in cold rivulets from throat to belly. This Granite, whoever he really was, had a plan.

'What's this about?' he asked.

'Do you enjoy life at Fenton Lodge?' asked Granite.

'Yes,' said Jacob. 'We've got good friends there and we're really well looked after.'

'But not free,' said Granite.

A few seconds of silence followed.

'We're happy there,' insisted Jacob. 'And it's time we got back.'

'Have you ever thought of how you'll feel about it in, say, three or four years' time?' asked Granite, leaning across the table and fixing Jacob with a piercing stare.

'We won't be there then,' said Jacob. 'We'll be at university and getting jobs and so on.'

'Will you?' Granite smiled, a little sadly, and tilted his head to one side. He took off the tinted spectacles and Jacob saw that his eyes were a startling blue. 'Do you really believe that, Jacob? Do *you*, Alex?'

We both know that's not going to happen, don't we? Alex sent to Jacob. *We'll be educated at Fenton Lodge— all the way through. They're not going to let us run off to Leeds or Bristol and get drunk in student union bars and start reading people's minds or mimicking them for a laugh.*

Shut up, sent back Jacob. *Don't speak. Not even in my head.*

'I think you both know that the British government is never going to let you go—not truly,' said Granite.

'Look—we can mimic and telepath a bit but it's not like we're Superman!' said Jacob. 'Some of the others . . .' he stopped himself before he talked about Gideon and Luke, who could move buses and hold back falling cliffs with their telekinesis, or Spook, who could panic people into a stampede with his terrifying, utterly convincing illusions. 'Some of the others have more impressive talents than us,' he concluded. '*They're* the ones who really might have a problem, but we're just a bit of a laugh. They'll keep tabs on us, of course—but we're not anything exciting to the Project.'

'I think you underestimate yourselves,' said Granite. 'But no matter—of course you must go back to your comfortable, secure, safe . . . prison.'

'It's *not* a prison,' said Alex. All the humour of the past few minutes had evaporated from his face and his eyes were, like his brother's, turning flat and stony.

'So—you're free to come and go?' queried Granite.

116

'Well—no—but that's what most boarding schools are like!' argued Alex.

'So . . . in the holidays . . . you're free to come and go then?' persisted Granite. 'Your family—they can turn up and take you off to tea at any time, can they?'

No, thought Jacob, *they can't. Not without clearance and minders and* . . . He sighed. This man clearly knew what he was talking about. 'What's your point?' he asked.

'My point, Jacob, is that you are never going to be free. Not like me. Not like Olu. Not all the while you're meekly submitting to the rules at Cola Club. And . . . maybe that's fine by you. And if it is, pay no more attention to me.' He sat back in his seat and raised both palms. 'If you're both happy with your lives, then that's fine. But . . . think on this. You are not normal human beings. You have *never* been normal human beings, and so the rules of other normal human beings really do not apply.'

'We *live* in a world of normal human beings,' said Alex. 'We can't change that.'

'No—but you can play it,' said Granite, a slow smile spreading across his face. 'Imagine the fun.'

'Play it?' said Jacob. 'How?'

'Well, like Olu does. His power means he cannot be held—cannot be chained, imprisoned. He is free. So why should he worry about getting GCSEs and A Levels and a job and a mortgage and a nice little starter flat in the grubby end of town? If you won the National Lottery would you carry on cutting out ten-per-cent-off coupons?'

'But—we're not above the law!' said Jacob. He glanced down, uncomfortably, at the new clothes Olu had given him last night. Alex had on a different set today—jeans and a jade green sweatshirt and expensive trainers. They'd found more gear in their room after breakfast in Dominica that morning. Their friend had clearly nipped out 'shopping' again. 'Olu . . . steals things.'

'Because he has to, to survive!' said Granite. 'And it's not as if he's mugging grannies, is it? Supermarkets throw out 100 times the food one skinny Olu needs every day. It's a drop in the ocean. And anyway, Olu can get money and pay whenever he feels like it.'

Jacob and Alex both suddenly realized that Olu, of course, could be the world's best bank robber. He'd only need to port into the vault!

'So—do you rob banks?' asked Alex, turning to stare at their new friend.

'Nah,' said Olu. 'Can't. Well—I could do the cashiers' end easy enough—but I don't like screaming people. The bank vault would be cool but I've never been inside one, and I have to have seen it to port into it, remember?'

'Sadly,' said Granite, 'they don't do tourist trips around the Bank of England vaults or print postcards of the interior. If they did, we'd be multimillionaires, wouldn't we?'

'Bank robbers is what you'd be!' said Jacob.

Granite smiled again. 'Your commitment to honesty and fair play is laudable, Jacob,' he said. 'How honest and decent do you think our banker friend here is?' He hit the PLAY button on the dock again and once more the hard, cut-glass voice rang out:

I don't care what excuses you've come up with today, Harris. I have a half hour window open at 2 p.m. and I expect you to be there. If you can't make it I shall assume you agree to the foreclosure and will instruct my people to proceed. Good day.'

Granite thumbed the machine off and looked around at all three of his guests. 'Peregrine

Carrington, OBE. His *bonus* this year was three million. He got it six months after making 3,000 staff redundant—and his greed and ineptitude has cost thousands of ordinary people their life savings. In any other job he'd be done for fraud. He has access to funds—right now—of over a billion. His bank is based in the City of London. He has a meeting today in . . .' he checked his watch '. . . just under five minutes. After that meeting he will be making a visit to the vaults. I'd like you, Jacob, to meet him.'

'What?' Jacob narrowed his eyes at Granite. 'How do you think *that's* going to happen?'

'Easily,' said Granite. 'I know the bank—I know the meeting rooms. I don't know the vaults but I know the route down to them. I've shown Olu all the pictures so he knows where and how to port in. He'll take you with him and then get Carrington out of the way while you get inside the vault.'

'I've told you—I don't have those kinds of powers!' insisted Jacob. He felt as if he'd got into a rollercoaster car without noticing and was suddenly powering towards a stomach-lurching drop with no idea how to stop it and get off. *Alex—we need to get out of this!* he sent to his brother. *Think of something!*

'Of course you have those kinds of powers!' said Granite. 'Carrington's way in is a voice recognition system. Any ordinary mimic, no matter how gifted, could never fool it. Nor could a recording—it's wired to recognize devices of any kind. But for you, Jacob—or you, Alex—a piece of cake!'

'What about the other security?' asked Alex. 'There'll be guards and cameras all over the place.'

'No guards at the point Olu ports in,' said Granite. 'It's too far in. And cameras? So what? Your brother will be in and out in seconds. With Olu beside him, nobody can possibly catch him.'

'Your brother,' asserted Jacob, with a serious look at Alex, 'Will not be in and out *at all*. I'm not doing this. And nor is Alex. We're not interested. Olu—it's time to go.'

Olu looked at Granite, one eyebrow raised. Granite seemed to be suppressing a smile. He inclined his head just slightly. 'Take Alex first,' he said. 'But give him your outer layer before you go.'

Olu got up and took off the pale blue zip-up hooded top he'd been wearing. It was fleecy and warm inside. He handed it to Alex. 'Go on—put it on. It'll be cold . . . taking you back.' He glanced at Jacob, who was on his feet, filled with uncertainty

121

and fear. Something was wrong here—but *what* exactly? 'S'OK, Jake,' grinned Olu. 'Chill, bro! I'll be back for you in two ticks!'

Alex looked at Jacob as he shrugged his arms into Olu's top. *I don't like this,* was all he had time to send before Olu grabbed his wrist and Jacob, Granite and the house were gone.

Alex felt himself slam down on something hard, unforgiving and chilled, like the inside wall of a fridge. 'OLU!' he yelled. 'Where have you taken us?' But his voice seemed to whip away from him as soon as it got past this throat. There was wind around him—a steady, sharp, cutting wind. His hair was flying straight out from the top of his scalp as he crouched, trying to deal with the dizziness. His third teleport today was obviously too much because it felt as if the very ground beneath him was swaying.

Alex opened his eyes and tried to sit, but the swaying only got worse. Just above him, Olu yelled in his ear, 'Better not get up! Just stay flat . . . and really, *really* still. Don't worry—it won't be for too long! Jacob won't let you freeze to death!'

Alex twisted his head around just in time to see Olu vanish. Still the swaying did not stop and he grabbed for a metal strut just to his right. Above him were some kind of mechanical workings—a short curved boom of criss-crossed metal, which made him think of Meccano, reaching just two or three metres above his head and connecting with some wheels and pulleys, anchored across two metal cables, one thick and one thin.

Alex was shaking so hard he could feel the movement reverberating through the metal floor under his shoulders, hips and elbows. Although his brain fought valiantly to stop him coming to the only possible conclusion—*It can't be! You're dreaming this! It's just a side effect of too much porting!*—all too soon there was no option but to turn over and slide his face over the finely iced, smoothly curved edge.

Below him was a thousand feet of nothing. He was lying on the roof of a cable car.

16

'You've really got him,' Jacob said to Granite. 'He'll do anything for you, won't he?'

Granite twisted the silver ring on his left hand and smiled at Jacob. 'Loyalty is a rare and wonderful thing. His father was a thug. Little wonder he bonded with *me*.'

'No . . .' said Jacob, 'it's more than that.'

And he knew he was right because for just a fraction of a second, just as Olu had vanished, Granite's shutters had wobbled—like a Venetian blind in a sudden gust of wind. Jacob had seen *something* going on in his head. Something dark and gleaming . . . he could not yet work it out. He knew it *meant* something important. But that was as far as he'd got.

And then Olu was back. 'Ready?' he said, grabbing Jacob's arm.

Granite gave a little wave, but he didn't say goodbye.

Because it wasn't goodbye.

Jacob realized this as soon and he and Olu arrived. They ported into a shock of freezing air—in a small hut, somewhere high up. Jacob could *smell* the altitude the moment they arrived. He gripped a wooden banister and stared all around him; getting his bearings quickly this time.

'How come I'm not surprised?' he murmured, coldly. He turned, taking in the cables, the huge wheels and cogs above his head, the flat grey concrete platform, and the warning signs in French and German. 'You *didn't* take me back to Fenton Lodge after all!'

'Sorry, mate,' said Olu, standing close beside him. 'It's for your own good—and for Alex's . . . You'll thank me later!' He guffawed as the parental phrase left his lips.

'Where is Alex?' growled Jacob.

'It's OK—he's just over there!' said Olu. He pointed out of the hut and down the mountain, along many metres of taut metal cable, to a small, red box hanging high over the grey-white valley. The empty cable car was not travelling along the line but swinging from side to side in the wind. On top of it clung a small figure in a blue hooded top.

'ALEX!' yelled Jacob—sending the cry to his brother's mind at the same time. *ALEX! Are you OK?*

There was a sickening lurch in his belly as his brother's vertigo spun back across the thin air between them. *I've had better days.*

Jacob twisted and grabbed Olu by the throat. He slammed him up against the concrete wall of the hut and bellowed into the boy's shocked face. 'Get him off there NOW!'

Olu's eyes bulged. He croaked something, Jacob let his throat go and was instantly staring at nothing.

'Cool it!' Olu stood at the far end of the cable car hut, rubbing his reddening neck and looking offended. 'As long as he holds on he'll be just fine.'

'Get him OFF there! NOW!'

'I'll get him really soon.' Olu checked his watch. 'In about . . . ten minutes. That's all the time it should take to do Granite's plan.'

'Why? Why have you got to do Granite's plan?!' demanded Jacob. 'What hold has he got on you?!'

'Hey—Granite's cool! He knows best, man!' protested Olu. 'After my dad died there was nobody else in this world who gave a damn about me. I owe him. And anyway, he's right. You and Alex—you're just prisoners. We're trying to help you escape.'

Alex was scrabbling closer to the metal arm of the cable car now, as a strong blast of wind shook the suspended vehicle. Even from here, Jacob knew his brother's eyes were screwed shut as he tried to hold off terror and despair. *Hang in there!* sent Jacob.

Nice choice of words! Alex sent back. Jacob was glad he had a sense of humour left.

'You're wrong,' said Jacob, turning back to Olu. 'About many things. Oh—and by the way—I know your dad didn't just "die". I can see right into your head. You took him to a desert and watched him have a heart attack in the dunes. Nice one, Olu. Nice.'

Olu looked angry for the first time since Jacob had met him. 'You don't know anything about my dad—or me. And if you want to get your brother back in one piece, shut up and do what Granite says.'

He strode over and reached for Jacob, and Jacob deflected him with an elbow strike to the shoulder, before punching him hard in the gut. Olu staggered back, bent over, coughing. 'Fine,' he gasped. 'Have it your way.' He vanished.

It took only seconds for Jacob to realize the folly

of his violence. How was he ever going to get Alex to safety without Olu?

But after a minute the boy was back. 'Worked out how much you need me, yet?' he asked, his arms folded and his face hostile.

Jacob resisted the intense urge to bodyslam him to the floor. 'Fine. I'll do it.'

'Now you're getting it,' said Olu. 'Come on, then.'

This time Jacob allowed him to grab his wrist and a second later they were back in the warmth of Granite's house. Jacob didn't protest when he saw the man. There was no point and, more importantly, no time. 'Your plan,' he said, fixing Granite with a cold stare. 'Run through it now. And we go.'

'Smart boy,' said Granite.

17

There was next to no dizziness this time—even though this was his fourth port in less than an hour. Perhaps because he was getting used to it, perhaps because he was so full of rage there was no space for it. Most likely Olu had made up the 'three port limit' rule as an excuse to keep them both overnight. They arrived in a corridor of pale green glass walls and woodblock floor. Behind them was a sealed airlock door, its panel of lights still flashing from the recent entry of one Peregrine Carrington. In front of them, his back turned and striking out for another sealed airlock door at the far end of the corridor, was the man himself, wearing a dark pinstripe suit and carrying a leather attaché case.

Olu and Jacob followed him, taking no trouble to be quiet. Carrington spun around. When he

129

saw two teenage boys, his pale brown eyes widened and his mouth dropped open, revealing a set of expensively veneered teeth. 'How the hell did *you* get in here?' he demanded, affronted rather than afraid. Jacob hopped into his head and easily picked up the man's wild conjecture about sons of staff or a school visit gone wrong . . . both of which were rejected instantly, for staff could *never* bring children in and a school visit here was unheard of.

Olu nudged him. 'Go on,' he said.

'How the hell did *you* get in here?' said Jacob. He watched the man's face morph from confusion and annoyance to total astonishment as he heard his own voice played back across this young boy's tongue.

'Who are you? What is this about?' he demanded. 'Security is already alerted. You're in a lot of trouble.' He nodded towards a camera on the angle where the ceiling met the wall.

'Who are you? What is this about?' said Jacob. 'Security is already alerted. You're in a lot of trouble.' And then, as Olu strode towards the shocked banker, Jacob turned quickly and stared into the camera.

'Keep your head down,' Granite had instructed. 'It's no big deal but you may as well do what you can to avoid being identified.'

That was one instruction Jacob was determined to ignore. He looked right into the camera and mouthed six very distinct words at it, before turning back to Olu and Carrington, who was attempting to get away from him in front of the sealed airlock door.

'Go on,' said Olu, grinning. 'Just say the password and go on through!'

'I'm not an idiot!' said Carrington. 'And *you* are about ten seconds away from a young offender's institution, young man.'

'I'm not an idiot,' repeated Jacob, but he didn't bother with the rest because Olu had grabbed Carrington's arm and man and boy were gone.

Alone in the glass corridor, Jacob walked towards the door and examined the brushed steel panel beside it. A red light pulsed next to a button with V R ENTRY engraved on it. He pressed the button and an automated female voice announced: 'State name and date.'

'Peregrine Carrington,' said Jacob in the slightly nasal cut-glass voice of the original. He thought for a while and then added the date, noting with wonder that less than twenty-four hours had elapsed since this 'adventure' had begun. There was a hiss and the red light turned green as the curved airlock door slid around, then a small punch of displaced air as Olu ported back and followed Jacob through.

'Don't waste time searching the drawers,' Granite had said. 'You'll have only thirty seconds or so before security arrive. Olu could port them out of the way, of course, but that would be tiresome, so get a move on and just get some currency. You'll find the notes in wrapped bundles, stacked like bricks.'

This was exactly what they did find. The vault's walls were covered with closed metal cabinets but the currency was just sitting there, on the concrete floor. The stack was resting on some kind of trolley and the amount of money within it was mind-boggling. There must have been 200 fifty-pound notes to a bundle. Jacob grabbed a dozen or so, his brain calculating wildly . . . 200 times fifty times twelve . . . that had to be—what—£120,000 in his arms?

'Woo-hoo!' said Olu. 'Happy days.'

'Where did you take Carrington?' asked Jacob.

Olu hooted with laugher. 'To a pub in Brixton.

You should have seen his face. He didn't exactly fit in there.'

'No heart attack then?' Jacob asked, eyeing Olu without humour.

'He's fit enough to enjoy a beer.' Olu grabbed one armful himself before reaching across for Jacob's shoulder, his face clouded. 'Let me show you something.'

Two seconds later Jacob could barely breathe. The heat was so intense. 'Here you go,' said Olu, shading his eyes. 'Here's where my dad died.'

Jacob screwed up his face against a sudden slam of sand, gusting on hot, hot air. He spluttered and turned his back into it. As soon as he could open his eyes again he made out the dunes, stretching away endlessly under a blue, blue sky. His feet, in their stolen deck shoes, were sinking through the hot upper layers to cooler granules below.

'What are you *doing?*' he bellowed at Olu. 'Why have you brought me here?!'

'Just thought you'd like to see,' said Olu, shrugging. 'The place where you think I killed him.'

'I didn't say you'd killed him,' spat Jacob, trying to get the sand out of his mouth. 'I said you watched him die.'

'Only after I'd tried to save him,' said Olu, and even here, in the blinding yellow light of the desert, Jacob could see the haunted look in his eyes. 'I didn't mean for him to die. He just wouldn't let go of me. He had me by the throat and he was smashing my face in. I couldn't breathe. I had to port and he had to come with me. It was him or me.'

Jacob said nothing. He picked up the truth of Olu's story and some violent flashes of memory. There was no doubting that the boy's father had been a brute. But so what? He couldn't get into this now. There was no time for it. 'Look, Olu—I believe you! And I get why you're doing stuff for Granite—he's a proper father figure and all that— but you don't have to do everything that he tells you to! You can get me and Alex back home *now*, can't you?' Jacob felt sweat trickle down between his shoulder blades and every breath he took was like inhaling at an open oven door.

'I *could*,' said Olu. 'But I won't. Trust me, Jacob— Granite's the best thing that ever happened to me. And he could be the best thing that ever happened to you, too, if you gave him a chance.'

Jacob flung the money into the sand and grabbed Olu by the shoulders, shoving his face close. 'I don't *like* him!' he grunted. 'He's devious and calculating . . . and he's playing *you*, too!'

'Pick up the money,' said Olu, stonily, pushing him back. 'Or I'll leave you behind.'

Jacob retrieved the cash and then they were back in Granite's house, a sandy avalanche of cash bundles dropping to his thick chocolate-coloured carpet.

'Nice work!' said Granite.

'Two hundred grand,' shrugged Jacob. 'I would have thought you'd want more.'

'Aah—but we *have* more, don't we? Now that you've got Olu inside the vault, he knows where it is and what it looks like. He can get in again any time—without further need of your services, Jacob. Nicely done. Thank you.'

'Alex,' said Jacob. 'I want him back here now!'

'Of course you do,' said Granite. 'And so do I. A terribly cold place to leave the poor chap. First though . . . there's just one more thing I need you to do for me.'

Jacob felt his heart plummet. This was a nightmare. He was absolutely trapped. What now? The Crown Jewels?

***

The roof Alex was lying on was about the width and length of his bed back at Fenton Lodge. His treacherous mind replayed again and again the view over the edge of it. The valley below was almost impossible to place on any scale because it was just white and black—snow on rock. But there were trees too, running across the steep slopes like dark green veins, which gave him some idea. All Alex knew was that if he fell it would be a long time before he hit the ground. Long enough for a *lot* of his life to flash before his eyes.

His fingers were so cold they could barely move, but he eased one hand off the metal struts so he could work his fingers before they froze permanently. The cable car was disused. Alex had worked this out from the state of the pulley and wheels above him. They were rusted into place on the cable. It was obviously some time since this mountain resort had seen a skier. Easing up just a little he could see, about two thirds of the way down the valley, a blue building—the cable car alighting platform at the base. He could pick out no sign of life—no passing caretaker who might spot the distant blur of a stranded boy and call out mountain rescue.

He *had* to believe Olu would come back. He *had* to. What had he said? 'Jacob won't let you freeze!' So, obviously, they were blackmailing Jacob into that bank job by threatening his little brother. Alex felt a sour twist in his belly. He had told Jacob, just last night, that they should enjoy this 'adventure'. Now he felt like such an idiot. Jacob had been suspicious of Olu from the start—and Alex had too. So why had he gone along with the boy?

But then—what choice did he or Jacob ever have? Olu held all the cards. If you could just step into another dimension and pluck out what you wanted—animal, mineral or vegetable—why wouldn't you? It's not as simple as that, though, is it? his mind argued. Olu needs something too— he needs something that Granite gives him. What's different about Granite? Why does Olu care about him? Because he isn't fazed by Olu's power? No. It's more than that. Jacob's picked up something more, too, I know. But what?

He remembered Olu explaining how Granite was so named because he was 'his rock'—the only one Olu could not *force* to teleport. So . . . what?

Was this some kind of parental boundary thing? Did Olu really adore Granite just because the man had some ability to resist him? No . . . a strong parent didn't just 'resist' their child's wilfulness—a strong parent actually stopped it.

Jacob, he sent. *I think it's not just that Olu can't make Granite teleport. I think Granite knows how to stop Olu too.* As soon as he sent the words Alex felt a rush of conviction. He did not know the detail—but he knew his guess was right.

The sending had calmed him a little too. He felt something buffet back from Jacob—a sense of anger and frustration. Yep—that was Jacob! They were still in touch, no matter how many thousands of miles were currently between them.

And then it occurred to Alex that there were other senders too. And other receivers. *You know what, Lisa,* he spun out, conversationally, into the ether, *it's really about time you put a bit of effort in and found me.*

And there, 2,505 metres above sea level, plastered flat to the swinging roof of a rusting cable car in a deserted mountain range, Alex set up a Cola beacon.

18

Lisa Hardman slammed down her magazine and shouted a very rude word.

'Oh dear . . . feeling a bit haunted?' asked Gideon, not taking his eyes off the hand-held computer game he was mashing between his thumbs.

'Not very ladylike,' muttered Dax, peering over Gideon's shoulder.

Lisa gritted her teeth. 'It's fine for *you*! They don't ask *you* to stay on constant alert, day and night, for any kind of contact AT ALL! You can just chill out, can't you?'

Dax and Gideon looked at each other. Neither of them was in the least bit chilled out. Nor was any other thinking, feeling Cola at Fenton Lodge that day. Two of them had, after all, just disappeared. The shock of discovering that Jacob had now gone, possibly the same way as Alex, had filtered through the college overnight as operatives streamed in from Control and went into a frenzy of searching and questioning, and every psychic dowser and medium and telepath available was marshalled into a thorough and organized system of attempting to locate the lost brothers.

Chambers, normally so cool, looked grey and grim, snapping out commands to the military as he strode repeatedly between the Development basement and his office. Reinforcements from London were arriving every hour. The place was teeming.

Dax and Gideon, along with Lisa and Mia, felt the Teller brothers' disappearance more keenly than most, as they'd been with Jacob so soon after Alex had vanished. The brothers had been through so much with them over the past few years, they really *did* feel like family. And the Teller brand of fun, which did so much to lift everyone's spirits, was already horribly missed.

Lisa, though, *was* suffering uniquely. Most of the time she kept her shutters well and truly closed to keep out the endless stream of spirits from the hereafter who wanted her to pass on messages to the living. She opened them only at specific times—in Development sessions, where Sylv, her spirit guide, would help her from the other side by forcing the communicating spirits into something approaching an orderly queue. But now, at Chambers's request, Lisa had been channelling all night and all day. She looked fit to drop. Her long blonde hair was tangled from the number of times she'd run her fingers through it in anguish, her beautiful designer clothes looked crushed and damp from time spent screwed up in her common room armchair sifting through the ceaseless spiritual babble. Her patience—never in great supply—was all but gone.

'C'mon, Lees,' said Mia, stepping up behind her friend and smoothing down her hair. 'Take a break. Get Sylv to hold them back for an hour so you can sleep.'

Mia's soothing touch took down the volume of the cacophony in her head, but Lisa shook her head. 'I can't switch off! Not while everyone's going so crazy about Jacob and Alex. What if a message came and I didn't take it? Nobody would ever forgive me. And I keep . . . feeling something in my hands . . .' Lisa rubbed her fingers together, looking perplexed. 'Ever since the early hours of this morning. Something . . . dark . . . magnetic. It's really important but I don't know why.'

Mia took Lisa's hands to see if she could pick up anything from them—but she couldn't. It was obviously a psychic thing, beyond her reach. She sighed and wiped a hand through her own dark hair—which had a knot or two in it as well. She had barely slept either, worrying about their missing friends and picking up the vibrations of fear permeating relentlessly through the college. Colas disappearing. Twice. From right here in the lodge—the most protected space in Britain. How could that *be*? Who would be next?

'I'm going to see Chambers,' said Lisa, disengaging her hands and getting up. 'Don't follow me. It won't be nice.'

Dax, Gideon and Mia exchanged glances as she left.

'Can we do *anything* for her?' asked Dax.

'No,' sighed Mia. 'She won't switch off until she literally drops.'

'I can't believe none of the dowsers have picked up anything about where Jake and Alex are!' said Gideon.

'They *do* keep picking stuff up,' said Mia. 'But then it changes. One minute it's in the north—then in the south—the Caribbean—Iceland! It makes no sense. Like someone's playing games with us.'

'Well—they couldn't pick up Spook last month, either, could they?' said Dax, reminding them all that there had been a disappearance—equally unexplained—even before Jacob and Alex went.

'It's really scary,' shivered Mia, looking so forlorn that Gideon dropped his computer game and went to give her a hug.

'They'll come back—just like Spook did!' he said.

'Yes,' said Mia. 'But what if they come back . . . just like Spook has?'

There was a long silence. They all knew what she meant. True, Spook Williams—the Cola Project's most brilliant illusionist—had come back in one piece and seemed as arrogant and self-serving as he ever had before. But he had no memory at all of what had happened to him in those missing few days and there was definitely something different about him since then. Something odd and worrying which even Mia could not put words to. And Mia had spent the most time with Spook, helping him to recover from whatever mystery trauma he'd been through.

'Spook was a weirdo long before he disappeared,' muttered Gideon, releasing Mia from the hug. 'You shouldn't bother about him.' But he knew Mia would. Mia would *always* bother about Spook.

The secretary quickly stood up as Lisa strode into the lobby of Chambers's office. 'You can't come in here,' he stated, his reedy voice sharp and fearful. 'Not without an appointment.'

Lisa eyed his cheap suit with distaste and couldn't stop herself reading his thoughts. *Stuck up little madam . . . So impressed with herself . . . Too beautiful to be anything but utterly spoilt.*

'Thanks,' she grinned. 'I *am* beautiful, aren't I?'

'Oh for the love of—' he muttered, turning his back on her, as if that might stop her. 'Will you please respect my privacy?'

'Oh get over yourself,' said Lisa. 'By the way, everyone knows you fancy Chambers something rotten, but you're wasting your time. He's not gay.'

The man was still opening and closing his mouth in shock as Lisa thumped on Chambers's door. Chambers opened it, saw the state of his secretary

144

and raised one eyebrow at Lisa. 'Are you bothering Hector?' he asked.

'Hector's bothered enough without my help,' said Lisa, pushing past him.

Chambers made an apologetic face at Hector. He was well aware of the 'crush' but the young man was exceptionally good at his job and never overstepped the mark. He didn't deserve the Lisa Hardman treatment.

Chambers let the door close behind him and turned to his most powerful dowser and psychic. 'I do hope you've come here to give me some important news, rather than just harass my staff,' he said.

Lisa sat on his sofa and said nothing. She did not have any news. She really was not at all sure why she had come here. Except . . . She stood up and moved across to his desk and traced her fingers along the surface until she found the magnetic baubles on the black plinth. Here was something. But what? Waiting for understanding was like listening to a railway track singing of a far distant train. She knew it was coming . . . In the meantime, something else fell into her mind—and right out of her mouth.

'You're thinking about Louisa,' she said.

Chambers felt his shoulders stiffen. 'That's not the information I was after, Lisa,' he said.

'I know,' she said. 'You think it was your fault . . . but it was nothing to do with you. You were only a kid.'

He took a long breath and retrieved a silver ballpoint pen from inside his jacket pocket. He clicked the nib in and out several times without even being aware of it. 'I was hoping you'd come with some information about Jacob or Alex, rather than the urge to take a daytrip through my subconscious.'

'I can see lots of people in your head,' said Lisa. 'All of us . . . me, Dax, Mia and Gideon . . . and Spook and the Teller brothers . . . all of us. But there are so many more you've helped—or tried to. I can see Tyrone when he was a kid—whoa—he had some bad braces! I can see a boy called Freddy, roller-skating. How could you know *him*? That was half a century ago! . . . But it always comes back to Louisa . . .'

'OK—enough,' said Chambers, tucking the pen away. 'I have work to do. And so do you. Stay open—keep searching.'

'Wait,' she said. 'You're going to need these.' She plucked six dark spheres off the magnetic desk sculpture. They clung together, like metal grapes in her palm. She walked across to Chambers and pressed them all into his hand. Her dark blue eyes locked on his but there was something hazy and opaque about them, as if she was not present in her own head. 'In your pocket,' she said. 'Keep these in your pocket and do not take them out until you learn how to use them.'

He felt goosebumps sweep up his neck and shoulders as he took them. He shoved them into his jacket pocket where they weighed heavily against his hip. 'Any idea why I would *want* to use them?' he asked.

'None at all,' said Lisa, blinking and looking normal again. 'Sylv thinks it's important. She's showing me sand, too . . . and I can smell old brick.'

Chambers stared at her for several seconds, his face unreadable and his mind now shuttered. She shrugged, looking tired and remote. 'That's it. I'm done. Ooooh—pretty!'

He guided her to the door. 'Ignore what I said, earlier. Get some rest, Lisa,' he said. 'Tell Sylv to keep them off you for an hour. You hear me?'

'Hmmmmm, pretty . . .' said Lisa, and wandered out, hands loose at her sides. The secretary looked daggers right at her, but she didn't even notice. A flare had just gone off in her head. A flare in the sky between ice-capped mountains.

19

'If he ends up hurt, I will make you pay,' said Jacob, his eyes locked with Granite's. The man had changed into black clothes but was still in the same seat, unruffled as ever.

'I'd expect nothing less,' said Granite, with a regretful smile. 'I hope, in time, you'll see what happened here today differently . . . but I have my doubts. You're such a boy scout.'

'What next?' snapped Jacob. 'There's no time for this.'

'Indeed no,' said Granite, checking his watch and reaching once more for the MP3 dock. He tapped it a few times, seeking another track, and then played out the woman's voice once again. 'I want to you extrapolate a little from this,' he said, picking up a mobile phone from a shelf behind him. 'I have a script. You *can* deliver from a script can you?'

Jacob narrowed his eyes. 'Yes.'

'Good. Take a seat by me. Read it through first while I set up the call.'

Jacob glanced through the words as he took a seat next to Granite and felt his insides contract. He had no idea what the script meant but he knew this was another deceit, and possibly a worse one than the bank job. It was more . . . personal.

Granite dialled an international number. His thumb paused over the CALL button. 'You're nervous,' he said, 'which is good, because she *would* be nervous. This woman is contacting a man twenty years after she disappeared from his life. She badly needs to see him . . . to explain why she disappeared. She vanished at the age of fifteen and no trace of her was ever found.'

'What happened to her?' muttered Jacob.

'That's beside the point,' said Granite. 'She's back now. And she needs to speak to David. Follow the script but DO NOT sound as if you're reading it. I will be following the conversation and also directing you.'

'How? With sign language?' said Jacob.

Granite grasped his shoulder. *No,* he sent. *Like this.*

Jacob blinked in surprise and then felt his heart tumble further towards his boots. With their telepathy talent he had felt there was *some* edge he and Alex held . . . but if Granite could do it too . . .? And had he already been inside their heads? If so, Jacob hadn't sensed it.

Yes, I have a little ability, Granite was saying in a conversational tone in his head. A few feet away, Olu stared at them both from an easy chair, his brow furrowed, clearly not able to follow. *I can listen in on what's happening—you must let me direct. Now . . . off we go.*

He pressed CALL and after a few muted beeps there was a click and a curt, stressed voice spoke one word which made Jacob's heart lurch.

'Chambers.'

There was a long pause while his mind reeled and he literally swayed in his seat. The urge to shout out for help—to alert the one man who had the resources to find and save Alex, was so strong it took the wind out of him. Next to him Granite squeezed his shoulder and sent *Deep breath, Jacob. You can do this. Your friends will thank you one day. Please . . . the script.*

'Hello? Who is this?' Chambers said, his voice sharper now.

Jacob gulped, feeling guilt and misery steal over him. Unless he was mistaken about the kind of man David Chambers was, what he was about to say would cause untold trauma.

'David, it's me.' The voice was nervous, hesitant. Perfect.

There was a long, long pause on the other end of the phone.

'It's Louisa.'

There was another pause but Jacob could easily pick up the shock ringing across the miles through so much satellite static. Yet when Chambers's voice returned, it was steady.

'How did you get this number?'

This was the first off-script foray. Jacob felt Granite's push in his mind. 'I can't explain that now . . . but . . . I need to see you. It's important.'

Again, a long pause. An image of Chambers resting his head against the cool glass of his office window and gripping the sill hard with one hand, marshalling his breathing.

'Louisa who?' he came back eventually.

'Oh David, I'm so sorry,' Jacob told him, and

dear god, he *was*. He had never used his talent like this before and it felt utterly wrong. But still the counterfeit voice poured from his throat. 'That day . . . that day in the park. I tried to call to you; I tried to let you know what was happening but you couldn't hear me or see me.'

There was just a trace of a break in his voice as Chambers replied: 'What did happen, Louisa? Tell me.'

'I can't tell you by phone. We have to meet.'

'You surprise me.' The dry, sceptical tone was back. *He's not buying it!* Jacob sent to Granite, jubilant. *Oh yes he is,* Granite sent back.

'Remember where we used to meet on the beach, back at Scarborough?' Jacob went on. 'The place even Emma didn't know about?'

'I might do,' said Chambers.

'Can you get there today? Can you make it by four o'clock? Please David . . . I really have to see you. There's so much I need to tell you—to explain.'

'Why me? Why not your parents? Your brother? Don't you think *they* might like to know too?!' The anger and pain was unmistakable in Chambers's voice now. *Damn! Don't buy it! Don't fall for this!* Jacob willed, but he knew Chambers would not pick it up.

For all his perceptiveness and insight, the man had no psychic skills at all.

'So . . . that'll be the spot below the cricket club then,' Chambers was saying now.

Tell him no. He knows where you mean, sent Granite, his fingers clenching hard on Jacob's shoulder.

'No, David. You know where I mean. Please be there.'

'How do I—?' began Chambers, but Granite took the phone and ended the call.

As Granite released the grip on his shoulder Jacob stared at the table in front of him in silence.

'Are we done?' he said, at length.

'Almost,' said Granite. 'How long do you suppose it will take for Chambers to get to Scarborough?'

Jacob shrugged. 'I don't know. It's got to be at least three hours by road.'

'But forty-five minutes by air,' said Granite, rubbing his chin thoughtfully. 'Knowing Chambers, I imagine he will get a helicopter to drop him on the edge of the moors—there's a private airfield quite close to Scarborough. Then he'll get a car and go on alone.'

'*Do* you know him?' asked Jacob.

'Well enough,' said Granite. 'But I hope to know him better.'

'So is that what this has all been about? Using me and Alex to set up a meeting with Chambers?' Jacob shook his head. 'Why didn't you just port into his office and get him?'

'For many reasons,' said Granite. 'One—I've not seen inside the buildings at Fenton Lodge, only the grounds, and it would be a difficult exercise getting past all those highly trained,' he smirked, 'special operatives.'

'I don't think you've got the guts,' said Jacob. 'You like Olu to do all your dirty work for you.'

'Hey!' protested Olu. 'I'm my own boss!'

'Yeah—right,' said Jacob, giving the boy a contemptuous glance.

'I need to meet Chambers in a civilized, non-threatening environment—without a team of hand-picked special ops twenty seconds away,' went on Granite. 'I am more than capable of utilizing any number of smash and grab tactics, Jacob, believe me, but I prefer not to at this stage. I'm looking for a conversation, not confrontation. And as much as I would like to ask Olu to port Chambers to me the next time he's out strolling through the grounds, the lay of which I *have* been privileged to study, the manoeuvre would kill him. He has a metal plate in his skull—the result of a nasty skirmish in the Gulf some years ago. People with metal in their heads do not travel well with Olu.'

Olu winced. 'One bloke, right, had this steel pin in his jaw,' he remembered. 'He came through with me from a street market in Portugal to a beach in Australia. *CRACK!* Metal just boiled—split his face in half.'

'Well, that must have put a cloud across your day,' said Jacob, glaring at the boy with distaste.

'It *did*!' said Olu. 'It was horrible. And I never *asked* him to come.'

Jacob turned his back on Olu. 'What now?' he said to Granite. 'You *have* to send Olu to get Alex or he'll freeze to death.'

'Of course—very soon,' said Granite. 'Don't worry too much. Alex is a fit young man and it's the middle of summer, even in the Alps. It's not actually *freezing* at all. Just somewhat bracing. He could last hours if necessary—but it won't *be* necessary. Come now—just a short trip to Scarborough and then you and your brother will be back at Fenton

Lodge—I promise. I have no wish to keep you. I hope one day to see you again, when you come to *me* of your own volition, but not this way. I am not a kidnapper.'

Olu stood up. 'Want to go now?' he asked, chirpily. He seemed to have no shame at all. 'We can get ice cream before he shows up.'

Granite twisted his fingers in that odd way he had before, Jacob noted. And then he nodded. He picked up a black cap and the mobile phone and said, 'Let's go.'

Olu stepped up, grabbed both their wrists, and took them to the English seaside.

20

'I think we're being played with,' said Paulina Sartre. 'Somebody has found a way to scramble our signals.'

'You're saying that someone's hacked into the spirit world?' demanded Lisa.

'Something like that,' admitted the principal. The lines around her eyes were marked today. She had been up all night, marshalling twenty-seven teenagers of varying ability in the psychic hunt for Jacob and Alex.

'Well, I don't care. This is a real one! It's a psychic beacon—a flare! Sylv agrees with me!' insisted Lisa.

'You may well be right,' sighed Paulina Sartre. 'But I still need to convince Mr Chambers and the military men. You can't blame them—so far it's been the Caribbean, the North Atlantic, Iceland, the Sahara desert and now France *and* the North Atlantic. They've found nothing—except a pair of swimming trunks! Chambers won't send out another team unless we're certain we're right.'

'I am right.' Lisa glowered out of the window. 'I *know* I'm right on this one! Alex is in France. In a mountainous area—the Alps. And he's . . . sort of . . . floating.'

Paulina Sartre raised one eyebrow behind her spectacles and her grey eyes rested on Lisa for a moment. Lisa knew she was considering how this would go down with Chambers. 'Go back to the map and pinpoint the location and closely as you can . . . *if* the signal is still there in half an hour, I will pass this information on and we'll see what can be done.'

'We can't wait!' exclaimed Lisa. 'Maybe whoever has Alex and Jacob knows about us and knows they have to keep moving them to mess up our dowsing. That would make sense, wouldn't it?'

'From the North Atlantic to the Sahara and back again in less than ten minutes?' queried Paulina Sartre. 'Tell me how that makes sense, *cherie*.'

Lisa knew she was wasting her time. She strode out of the principal's office, slamming the door.

159

Paulina Sartre sighed and shook her head. At any other time Lisa would not have got away with flouncing out like that—but today was different. Paulina rested her head in her palms and willed her own powers to improve, if only for one day.

'Tree house—now,' said Lisa, as soon as she and Mia found Dax and Gideon outside. The best friends were having a knockabout game of tennis on one of the courts. One court along, Spook Williams was playing against his illusionist pal, Darren Tyler, and clearly playing to win.

Darren, though, turned away from their rally and came over to the edge of the fence. 'Any news?' he asked.

'Nothing useful,' said Lisa. She had no intention of giving any details to Darren. He was OK, but he made friends with people who weren't.

'Darren! I thought we were having *a game*!' shouted Spook. When Darren only glanced back with a little 'be right there' wave, Spook flung his racquet down and stalked across. He was dressed in immaculate white shorts and a T-shirt of some expensive designer brand, and the sweat on his scalp had sculpted his dark red hair into pronounced waves.

'What's new, Hardman?' he asked, resting a languid hand on the fence. As his amber eyes fixed on hers, Lisa, not for the first time, felt a sense of . . . *absence* . . . in him. A coldness.

'Nothing's new, Spook. Go back to your game,' she snapped.

'Mia—is there *anything* you can do to sweeten this sour lemon?' asked Spook, smiling at the healer.

'Leave her alone, Spook,' said Mia, softly, as Lisa stalked off with Dax and Gideon, and Darren went to retrieve the tennis ball. 'She's having a really tough time today. All the dowsers and psychics are; you know that.'

'And how about you?' Spook reached across and put a warm hand on top of Mia's. 'I bet she's draining you of energy. Don't get too close to her when she's like this.'

Mia stared at his hand and then back up into his eyes. She felt herself flushing. 'I know what I'm doing,' she mumbled.

'Hmmm. What's best for everybody, eh?' said Spook. And he lightly touched her pale cheek. 'Don't let the world eat you up, Mia.'

'MIA!' called Lisa. 'Come *on*!'

Mia ducked away from Spook, her heart rattling oddly in her chest. Of *all* the people here . . . why him?

In the shade of the tree house Mia joined Lisa, Dax and Gideon. Lisa had a battered atlas of the world under her arm and she opened it up. 'Here,' she said, pointing to a mountainous region on the edge of France. 'This is where Alex Teller is at the moment.'

'How can you be sure?' asked Dax. 'I mean . . . you said the locations kept changing. Is he still there now?'

Lisa closed her eyes and let her fingers hang in the air above the open book. Then she let them drop and, as always happened when she dowsed, a push in the air seemed to drive her hand down to a specific point on the map, her index finger, with its polished, almond shaped nail, aimed precisely and unflinchingly. 'Yes, he's still there. He's set up a beacon for me.'

'A beacon?' asked Gideon. 'What . . . like a sort of psychic flare?'

'Exactly,' said Lisa. 'It's something he will have been taught in Development. It hangs there—

really bright and strong—sometimes for hours, even days.'

'But you're sure *he's* still there too?' asked Mia. 'I mean . . . what if he set off this beacon and then got moved again . . . would it still be there even if he wasn't?'

'No, not if he's alive. The beacon is anchored to him. When I talk about beacons lasting for days I mean . . . days after people have died.'

Gideon gulped. 'So . . . he could be dead . . . but he's not been moved.'

'Not yet,' said Lisa. 'And he's not dead either. Nor is Jacob—although I don't know where Jacob is right now. He *was* in London a little while ago and then he was in the Sahara Desert and now . . . I can't pinpoint him, so I'm focusing on Alex.'

'So—is Chambers on his way there?' asked Dax. 'Is he sending a team to your map coordinates?'

'No,' said Lisa. 'Chambers isn't even *here* right now. He's gone off somewhere—probably on a wild goose chase to one of the places they *were* at but aren't at now. And Mrs Sartre says she'll pass on my latest information . . . *if* it's still the same in half an hour! She thinks we're being played.'

'What if she's right?' asked Gideon. 'Maybe you

are being played. I mean—London one minute and then the Sahara Desert the next? Come on!'

'No. I'm right about this one,' said Lisa. 'Nobody could fake Alex's psychic beacon. I would know. And that's why you have to help.'

Gideon and Dax exchanged glances, guessing what was coming.

'You have to fly to him, Dax,' said Lisa. 'And Gideon—you've got to push!'

'Are you sure about this, Lees?' asked Mia. 'It's such a long way . . . and it could be dangerous.'

'No,' said Dax. 'She's right. If we don't do anything and Alex and Jacob never get found, we'll never forgive ourselves. I'll fly. I'm the only one who can. And Gideon can give me a shove, like he did when I went to London for Lisa. He'll get me there really fast.'

'What about your tracker chips?' asked Mia. 'You know you'll be followed!'

'Good!' said Gideon. 'We *want* him followed! We want all the Cola Project help we can get. If they won't believe you and send a team, we'll just have to send them after Dax.'

Dax nodded. 'It's the best plan I can think of.'

'Wait here,' said Gideon. 'I'm getting Luke too.

With both of us pushing, you'll go twice as fast.

Lisa took Dax's hand and pulsed a visual into his mind. He could see a mountain pass; white and grey; rock, ice and thin snow—and vein-like schisms of dark fir tree forests. Lisa ripped out the page of the atlas as Gideon arrived back with Luke. 'Take this too. And . . . good luck! Hopefully a Control helicopter will be right behind you.'

'Luke's cool,' said Gideon, as the twins reached the platform. Luke, just like Gideon only with dyed dark hair and glasses, gave Dax a thumbs up. He didn't talk much.

'OK,' said Dax, clapping each twin on the shoulder. 'I'll get clear of the trees and circle once. When you see me go over the lake . . . push! Double whammy fast!'

'We'll give it all we've got, mate,' said Gideon, grabbing his brother's shoulder.

'Mind . . . the mm-mountains,' said Luke.

21

David Chambers tore along the A171 at unwise speeds. The sleek silver Mercedes 4x4 would be a magnet for any traffic police and experience had taught him that they gave chase first and noted the secret service plates *afterwards*. He could not afford to be stopped—he didn't have the time and he certainly didn't have the explanation. Not that he would be required to explain himself to any country coppers, of course, but Whitehall would want something from him on why he had gone AWOL during one of the Cola Project's most serious crises.

Commandeering a chopper to the private strip hidden high on the eastern side of the Yorkshire moors was one thing—his sudden departure by air would raise no questions at all in the current situation. And it was a relief to make such good speed. How did Louisa *know* he could reach her so fast? How did she know that he had such resources at his disposal? How did she know anything about him *at all*? It wasn't as if he went back to school reunions wearing a badge printed with *Scarily Senior in Government Top Secret Projects*. Most of his old friends had no idea what had happened to him. Many believed he'd gone to live in Australia; a rumour he'd circulated years ago.

So—how did Louisa know? And how did *he* know that this really was Louisa? The last time he'd heard her voice she was fifteen. And he'd heard nothing from her lips since then—just the endlessly looped fifteen-second answerphone message which he'd first heard in a police station while he was a suspect for Louisa's murder.

The memory still made him shiver. After all the amazing and horrifying things he'd experienced in the intervening years, what still chilled him most was that memory—not of being accused of her murder, but of the moment when somebody actually said, *out loud*, that she was probably dead. Louisa. Glorious, funny, eccentric Louisa. His best friend since infant school, with her chunky brown plaits and her wide hazel eyes; the endlessly daft sense of humour and unstoppable kindness. To think that such an amazing lifeforce could have been snuffed out was unbearable.

'I'm going back the short way,' she'd said to him at the edge of the park. 'I'm late. You go and get your CD and bring it round later. Byeee.' And she'd waved at him and he'd caught her hand as it went by, wanting to pull her closer and behave like she was his girlfriend. After all, he'd been in love with her for at least three years, even if she had never noticed. But the fingers pulled away as her dog tugged her in the other direction.

The dog made it back. Louisa didn't. Everybody thought she'd been murdered. And he was the last person to speak to her so it was obvious he would be a suspect. Even after his alibi was proven—someone leaving the park had seen them part ways and then he'd been at a second-hand record shop before walking home with another friend from school— the tarnish never came off. Just being suspected seemed to be enough. None of her friends ever really spoke to him again afterwards.

Not knowing was the worst. After twenty years it still had the power to constrict his throat whenever he thought of it. He could only begin to imagine what her family had been through. He was certain that sometimes her parents had actually *wished* for a body to be found, just to end the torment. But Louisa's disappearance was as agonizing a mystery now as it had been back then.

Was that mystery going to be solved today? In the next hour? He found he was gripping the steering wheel so hard his knuckles were white. Was this *really* Louisa? His training told him no, it couldn't be. Not after all this time. But other instincts said yes—or else why was he here, now, when he should be back at Fenton Lodge masterminding the global search for Jacob and Alex Teller? Her voice . . . it was no longer that of a teenager, of course, but there were inflections and even that almost imperceptible lisp on certain words . . . The accent was exactly right; perhaps ironed out a little with travel and time, but still, right.

Goosebumps ran up and down his spine as the sea came into view. He hadn't been here for so long; his home town, clinging to the high red cliffs, all zigzag paths and gothic Victorian hotels. But he sped on to the less visited stretch of coast further south. He remembered well what he and

169

Louisa had found. It was a squat brick wartime bunker in the dunes which had been engulfed with sand and weeds when they'd discovered it. Together, one long damp summer, they had dug it out, careful to keep the high grass in place at the low concrete door, to hide their secret. The den they had made stretched inwards some four or five metres and downwards for half of that. They'd brought stuff to sit on—boxes and bits of carpet— and candles in jam jars. Louisa had brought chalk and drawn elaborate frescos of plants and animals by candlelight, while he had written out stupid comedy poems. They'd never shared it with anyone else.

The last time he'd been there was just before he left Scarborough for good. His family, still smarting from their son's false arrest, moved him to Bristol that autumn—to a fresh start. The day before the removals van came he had spent entirely in the beach-fort den, staring at Louisa's drawings and willing her to suddenly arrive, as if the past three nightmarish months had never happened. He had checked the fort, of course, within twenty-four hours of her disappearance; had gone back there daily for weeks as the shocking news of a girl's disappearance gradually became less shocking. Just history. Sad, unresolved, history.

At the lay-by which led down on to the footpath to the sea, he parked and got out of the 4x4. The familiar smell of summer-cooked vegetation and the tang of the sea was like an awakening ghost. He had a sense that his life might be about to twist on its axis. And maybe never twist back again.

OK.

It was a small response. Just two syllables, but Alex was certain it came from Lisa. It carried all her impatience and frustration. She had picked up his beacon. The only trouble was . . . Olu could show up at any time and port him off somewhere else.

As terrifying as his situation was, he now realized that his best hope was staying here until help arrived from Control. But where *was* he? How long would it take, even if they flew here in planes or helicopters? He could be in Switzerland or Austria, France—even Alaska! He shuddered to think how long he would wait for rescue if *that* was true. The relentless wind whipped at the back of his head and shoulders. He was back up in a sitting position, clinging tightly to the metal struts of the cable car arm, numb with cold. He had to *do* something. Sitting here getting hypothermia wasn't helping anyone. He had to take action! A strong gust of wind made the car tip and sway and the workings above his head sung out a low, metallic note, but he gritted his teeth and refused to give in to panic. *Think,* he told himself. *What can you DO? How can you get some control?*

He took a deep breath and forced himself to look around. He could make out several peaks through patches of mist. The snow clung to them in patches with areas of rocky grey showing through in places. At the foot of the valley were dark green seams of fir forest. He could also see the cable car alighting hut at the top of the mountain. It was closer to him than the base hut—but still a good half a kilometre away. There was no hope of climbing along the cables to get to it.

What about the car itself? Could he get inside it? He looked at the smooth curved edges of the roof and shuddered. Just putting his head over the drop would make him spin out of control. And besides, he had no idea how safe the floor of the car was—if it was wooden it could have rotted; if it was metal it

172

might have rusted through. He didn't even know if the windows could be opened.

What if there was safety equipment in it, though? Harnesses to travel down the line? Flare guns? There might be! He imagined himself finding a harness with a clip which could attach to the cables—speeding down as if he were on a zip wire. He could get to the base hut and find a telephone—get himself *out* of danger and maybe send a message to Jacob to let him know. Because Jacob was certainly being made to help Granite against his will. Alex had no doubt of it. It would be wonderful to take away the man's leverage!

But the drop! The vertigo! Still, the thought needled at him and as the minutes ticked on he realized he was going to *have* to look over the edge and see if there was a way into the car through a window. If he went over on the side where the suspending arm of the car was attached, he could lock his leg through the struts as he tipped. He couldn't fall if he did that, could he?

For another ten minutes his common sense battled with his fear. Why should he just sit here, waiting for Olu, when he might be able to escape? He should at least *try*! Finally the moment came.

He took several slow, deep breaths, controlling the panic. Then he worked his way around the cable car roof on his belly. The metal arm met one side of the roof of the car and arched up over the cables and the wheels in an elongated C shape. The gaps between the struts within it were big enough at the base for him to hook one leg through. He shoved his right foot in and hooked his knee around the metal. Above him the workings gave a little groan but he resolved not to hear it. Now, with his left leg under the right, able to move to cantilever his weight, and his right hand gripped rigidly on the struts, he eased towards the edge and, eyes closed at first, allowed his head to extend beyond it. He knew that he would have to deal with the dizziness for a while as soon as he opened his eyes, so he got ready for it with some more deep, controlling breaths—and then looked.

A long, desperate shriek of primal fear went off in his head. The drop was enough to reduce him to a screaming toddler. Nothing below him. *Nothing nothing nothing nothingohdeargodnothingatall* . . . only a bird flitting many metres below, oblivious to the horrified human dangling, so wrongly, up here in its world.

It was all he could do to keep control and not scramble desperately back to the other side of the metal struts and cling there, frozen, for ever.

ALEX! A shout from Jacob. He must have picked up the shriek, however far away he was. His telepathic voice sounded full of dread.

It's OK. I'm OK! he sent back, immediately, and felt the panic in his brother ease down a notch before the link was lost again. He wanted to hear more—to send more—but Jacob was so far away and the link was so weak. Only the most extreme emotions and the words that rode them seemed to be getting through. And he needed to focus anyway. No more freak outs. What was the point of all this if he didn't at least look inside the car?

He kept his eyes away from the drop and allowed them to travel the side of the car. It was covered in peeling red paint and its windows, blasted by years of rough mountain weather, were hard to see through. Inside was dim. There might be a cupboard with supplies—but he couldn't see it. He couldn't see any obvious way to open the windows either. The bird went past again, closer, distracting him and drawing his eyes back to the drop. Oh no . . . His head began to spin. He gripped on tightly with his right hand, the other sliding over the edge to his left, slippery with condensation and his own panicky sweat. His left elbow followed, slick and fast as the weight of his upended head pulled his shoulders around. A huge gust suddenly slammed into the car, making it swing violently, and as he scrabbled to pull himself back up his legs slid too, and the momentum of his dangling upper body against the sudden jerk of the car moving in the other direction tugged hard at his knee lock. A second later only his ankle was still hooked around the struts.

He was going to fall.

22

'He's going to fall.' Jacob's voice was flat and thin like cardboard.

Granite put a hand on his shoulder and a peculiar double emotion hit Jacob. His first instinct was to punch the man, hard, right in the centre of his face. He could actually visualize the blood spurting out of Granite's nose as he staggered backwards.

Yet at the same time there was a sense of peace swiftly travelling through him, calming his anguish. How could that be? To take comfort from the man who was putting his brother through such horror . . . it was repellent to even think of it.

'He's fine,' said Granite.

'Make Olu go and get him! Make him check!' said Jacob, shaking off the man's disturbing touch.

'I can't make Olu do anything,' said Granite,

twisting his ring on his finger and glancing across to where the teleporter sat, a few feet away in the grassy dunes. 'I can only suggest—and I would, truly, but we need him here now. Chambers may arrive any second. In half an hour this will all be over. Maybe Olu will take you for a little holiday in the Maldives before you go back to your studies. That'll warm your brother up. I hear it's exceptionally lovely there.'

Jacob gaped at the man. He must be insane. And yet he did not look or act it, and nothing of what little Jacob had been able to pick up from him telepathically suggested that Granite was mentally unbalanced.

'Olu—we're about to be in play,' said Granite, checking his watch and glancing back up the gorse covered sandy slope behind them. 'Port in to us on my signal, but keep your head down until then.' Olu nodded and vanished, reappearing a second later down at the water's edge, a good five-minute walk along the strata of dark red rock which had emerged with the receding tide.

'Time to go in; he'll be here any moment,' said Granite.

'I don't know what you think you're going to

achieve,' muttered Jacob. 'He'll know it's a trick as soon as he sees us. This is pointless.'

'No, it's not,' said Granite. 'There is very much a point to it, Jacob—one that will serve you well in future. I know you don't understand this, but the help you're giving me is *for* your friends at Cola Club. They will thank you one day.'

Jacob gritted his teeth as they clambered down over the edge of the old bunker. It was an aged brick-built thing, covered in weeds and sand. He would never even have known it was there, but Granite had led him directly to it. They pushed the weeds to one side and stooped under the low concrete lintel of the narrow doorway. Inside, the air was stale and old. It was dark. No light came in other than the narrow shaft through the doorway behind them. Outside the day was bright and warm but the temperature was cool in here.

'Into that far corner please,' said Granite. Jacob understood why he'd got changed. In his black shirt, trousers, and boots he was very hard to see. The black cap hid the gleam of his white hair. The glasses were gone and underneath the peak, in the shaft of light from the door, his eyes glowed ferociously blue. Jacob had thought the black look was all for effect but now he realized that Granite wished to remain in shadow, unseen—at least for a while. Jacob's clothes were fairly dark, and, backed away into the far corner behind Granite, he was pretty much invisible too.

Granite reached his left hand behind him and wrapped cool fingers firmly around Jacob's wrist. *Stay still and say only what I tell you to say,* he ordered, telepathically. And again he sent *calm* with it, and Jacob, resentfully, felt its effect. He also felt metal. The ring on Granite's finger. And shortly after it made contact, Jacob began to realize why that ring had been nagging at his mind. Finally, it gave up its story . . .

David Chambers felt sand work its way into his Italian leather shoes and right through his fine wool socks. He had not dressed, that morning, for a visit to the seaside. How flimsy life was, he reflected. So shiny and slender and terrifyingly easy to crush. He had learned many techniques over the years to stay strong and robust in the face of danger—handling everything from terrorists to biological warfare to natural disasters. Some of the experiences he had been through had left others around him with ruined minds. All he had ever believed in had been tested and twisted and flipped over and recalibrated, again and again. The Colas were only part of that. Long before he'd met his first Cola, he had been involved in some of the UK's best kept, most panic-inducing secrets. He had seen the impossible; used it for the country's own ends; set up the system of working with the dangerous and the miraculous; even looked into the face of an alien and nearly lost his senses for ever.

So, yes, David Chambers, for most of his adult life, was known as a man who could handle pretty much anything.

Anything but this. Louisa. Come back from the dead. He felt fifteen again. Desperately unprepared for any outcome at all.

The old fortification had been entered. He could tell, even after all these years, just by looking at the angle of the thicket of marram grass and sea bindweed across the low doorway. He pictured Louisa, scrabbling away with her hands, chucking sand in his face in her excitement, more than two decades ago. Had she scrabbled sand again just today?

Chambers scanned the beach, noting the handful of people on it—all some distance away. The nearest was some teenage kid poking about in a rock pool, facing out to sea. Nobody was watching. He walked quietly to the hidden entrance, pulled back the vegetation and stepped inside.

For a few seconds he just stared into the blackness, inhaling the familiar musty scent, his heart quickening in his chest. And then she spoke.

'David. I *knew* you'd come.'

Of all the reactions he'd expected, losing the strength in his knees was not one of them. David Chambers sank to the cold sandy floor, taking in a lungful of air. He couldn't even speak. He also couldn't see her. He waited for her to step into the light and rest a hand on his head; to kneel down in front of him and look into his eyes.

But she did not emerge from the shadows. At last he spoke, unable to disguise the shake in his voice. 'Where are you?'

'I'm here,' said the voice, and he detected something agonized in it. 'Just . . . stay there . . . don't come to me yet. I can't deal with it. Please . . . wait a moment.'

Chambers felt his senses prickle. Something was wrong here. Suddenly he sensed that there were more than two people involved in this reunion.

'Why are we here, Lou?' he asked. 'What happened to you? Why did you disappear?'

'I will explain,' she promised. 'But there's someone you have to meet first. Someone who helped me find you.'

Chambers squinted as his eyes became more accustomed to the gloom and a figure moved towards him. He reached into his jacket pocket for his small halogen torch.

'He needs to talk to you and . . . oh god I'm so sorry, I'm so sorry, Mr Chambers, I had to do this. I had to do it for Alex.'

Chambers let out a dry bark of humourless laughter. He had known, if truth be told, from the second she did not come to him. His hopeful heart slammed shut and his Cola Project personality slid back into place a second later. Even before he switched on the torch he was shaking his head and sighing, 'Jacob . . . it's all right. I will sort this out.'

And then, with a click of his thumb, there was light bouncing around the old chamber and he found himself face to face with a white-haired man, smiling and directing a pure blue gaze of amusement at him.

'Well,' said Chambers. 'This is a surprise.'

'Isn't it?' beamed the man, leaning in towards him conspiratorially, like an old friend.

'So . . . you're not quite as dead as we all thought,' said Chambers, mirroring the man's cross-legged sitting position and scanning the room for Jacob. He saw the boy standing rigidly in one corner, his face a mask of guilt and misery. 'Jacob—I promise, we will sort this out. You have nothing to apologize for. I know how this man works.'

'I never *said* I was dead,' said his opponent. 'I just never got around to correcting all the *reports* of my death.'

'What has he told you about himself, Jacob?' asked Chambers.

'Not much,' came back the reply. 'He's called Granite, but that's not his real name.'

'No,' said Chambers. 'He has quite a few names. We knew him as Marcus Croft up until his sudden "death" three years ago. He's a freelancer. Worked in British intelligence for a few years. Highly effective but somewhat . . . flawed.'

'So what does he want with you?' asked Jacob.

'Please sort it out because we have to get Alex back.'

'What have you done with Alex Teller?' snapped Chambers, leaning across to Granite or Marcus Croft or whoever he was.

'Relax, David, he's fine,' said Granite. 'And I will prove it to you in about five minutes. He will be right here in this room with us. Getting him safely back to you is very much part of my plan, you know.'

'Oh really? And what is the rest of your plan?' Chambers eyed Granite coldly, pressing the base of the torch down into the sand so that it shone an eerie uplight across all their faces.

'First, I wanted to talk to you alone, without a trail of special ops; without wires or bugs,' said Granite. 'And I apologize for using your long lost sweetheart as the tool for the job—but there was really nothing else I could find out about you which was quite so certain to get you here alone.'

'So—you hacked into the files, found out my personal history,' stated Chambers.

'Yes, I hacked in,' admitted Granite. 'And, I must say, I was quite moved. A really terrible start to your young adult life. No wonder you went into the special services—righting wrongs all over the world, tackling the more and more outlandish cases, always on the lookout, I imagine, for some old, cold trail which might explain what happened to Louisa Campbell.'

'How could you know about this place?' asked Chambers. 'This was never in any file.'

'No—but it was in your head, poor chap,' chuckled Granite. 'I saw it there often enough when we worked together. Didn't take too much working out. There aren't many old bunkers in these parts. David, I really do feel for you. This must be tough.'

Chambers eyed him coldly. 'Your sympathy is giving me a headache, Marcus. Let's move this along, shall we? What do you want?'

'It's not so much what I want,' said Granite. 'It's much more about what I can offer . . .'

23

The valley spun below him and gravity mercilessly pushed him towards it. Alex felt his right trainer snag against the strut as he was jerked down beside the window sill of the cable car. *Now* he could see inside properly as his upended head cracked against the glass. Inside was empty. But there wasn't much time to study it. His arms scrabbled vainly for a hand-hold. He could feel his right heel twisting free from the shoe. His whole body weight was dragging on it. Any second now he would plummet head first to the valley floor. He could feel his heel slip . . . and slip . . .

. . . *free* . . .

For a moment he seemed to float in the air, like a cartoon character walking unwittingly off the edge of a cliff. It was true what they said . . . time really did slow down as you went to your death.

Then there was another stomach-lurching shudder through his body as he *did not* fall. Something had stopped him. Something had caught his ankle.

'HANG ON! HANG ON, ALEX!' yelled a familiar voice.

It must be Olu, showing up to port him away again, just in the nick of time. He twisted his face up to stare at his rescuer and then gave a shout . . . which was really, at his angle, more of a gurgle . . . because it was *not* Olu.

It was *Dax Jones.*

Dax was flat on his belly, one arm and one leg hooked through the struts and one hand holding Alex's ankle. His face was crimson with the strain.

'Wait! We'll get you! Don't give up,' yelled Dax, his voice grating with the strain of Alex's entire, wind-buffeted bodyweight hanging from one arm.

Alex knew it couldn't work. Dax couldn't possibly pull him back up. A roaring, chopping, buffeting sound shook his head as his blood pounded through his ears. Soon, in spite of Dax's best efforts, he *would* fall, and as he reached terminal velocity the air resistance would probably rip the clothes from his body before he hit the ground.

'Tell Jacob . . .' gurgled Alex. 'I'm sorry . . . for getting him into this stupid adventure.'

The roaring and chopping got louder and flickering shadows passed overhead.

'Tell him yourself!' yelled another voice.

Alex saw an upside-down face, half a metre from his own. He thought maybe he was hallucinating. But the face was grinning and two arms, clad in red, were reaching for him. There was a thud as the man made contact, and whirring, clipping noises as a harness of some kind was attached to him.

'Got him!' yelled the man and raised one arm to the helicopter above them. 'Let go now, Dax, good lad!'

Dax let go of Alex's tortured ankle and shifted to a peregrine falcon, perching on the top of the rusted cable car workings as his friend was hoisted up. A few seconds later Alex was crumpled on the floor of the helicopter while the man slid the door shut and tipped his visor back. 'Are you injured?' he yelled, above the thunder of the engine. Alex shook his head, but a young paramedic began to check him over anyway. His ankle hurt and he was shaking with shock and cold, but he didn't think there was any real damage.

'I'm OK,' yelled back Alex, as a blanket was wrapped around him. And he *was*. Because now his mind was working furiously on a plan to rescue Jacob. But how could he steer the rescue when he had no idea where Jacob *was*? 'Listen—we have to *land*! Down *there*!' He pointed to the valley, far below. 'Can the pilot get us down there?'

His rescuer stared down and then went to speak to the pilot. Coming back after thirty seconds he nodded. 'Yes—there's an area he can land on. But why? We need to get you back to Fenton Lodge. You've probably got hypothermia!'

'Do this,' said Alex, gratefully accepting a pouch of warm, sweet energy drink from the paramedic. 'And you'll get me *and* Jacob back.'

Dax Jones was surprised to see the grey helicopter suddenly drop down into the valley. He stooped and dropped after it. By the time it had landed he had already shifted to a fox, sitting patiently in the snow, close to some trees. He would have shifted back to boy form, but it was damn cold and he needed the fur. Alex, wrapped in a thermal blanket, peered out of the chopper and motioned to Dax to get in. Dax made his way under the spinning chopper blades and into the aircraft, shifting back to boy form, reluctantly.

'Look—here's how it's got to go,' Alex was saying to Jem, the leader of the two-man special ops team. 'I was teleported up there by a guy called Olu.'

The special ops blinked and stared at each other and then back at Alex. Dax was less shocked. He had become used to extraordinary, mind-bending discoveries over the past few years.

'He's a Cola—but he wasn't found by the Project,' explained Alex. 'He can teleport all over the world and take people with him when he goes.'

'That explains *a lot*,' said Jem, his Scottish accent thickening with his surprise. 'We followed one tracker . . . to Iceland!'

'Yeah, I know,' said Alex, feeling rather ashamed of how he'd laughed about that just last night. 'And I bet the dowsers have been freaking out, picking us up all over the place.'

'They have been,' said Dax. 'Lisa was going mental because nobody would take her seriously. Then, this afternoon, she said you'd set up a beacon and you were definitely here. We just had to get here before you were gone again. I went AWOL to get to you, and trusty old Jem here took the initiative—and a helicopter—and followed my trackers.'

191

Alex grinned at Dax. 'You got here just in time. But look—the details will have to wait—Olu could port back any second to get me and if he discovers I've gone he'll just port away again—and then we'll never find a way back to Jacob. Olu *has* to find me.'

'You're never suggesting we pop you back up *there*, are you?' said Jem, raising his eyes up to the distant cable car. 'Because I'm not doing it!'

'No,' said Alex, with a shudder. 'I've got a better idea than that.' He glanced across to the drift of snow on the slope beneath the cable car—the spot where he would have landed and punched a hole right down to the bedrock if he *had* dropped. 'I need you to take me up in the chopper . . . and drop me there.'

'You what?' Jem looked unimpressed.

'Just high enough so that when I fall I will make the right shape in the snow—maybe roll a bit down the slope.'

'And the point of this *is* . . . ?'

'Just four or five metres should do it,' said Alex. 'It's got to look like I fell. Olu won't know the difference. And we'll need some digging gear . . .'

Jem looked at the paramedic. 'What do you think?' he asked her.

'I don't approve,' she said. 'But . . . he's recovered amazingly fast. As long as he's not in the snow for longer than twenty minutes, he'll be OK.'

Jem nodded and Alex's plan rolled out. While Dax hovered above, keeping a peregrine eye on the cable car for signs of Olu porting in, the helicopter rose a few metres over the snow drift and Alex Teller dropped out of it. He hit the soft snow and rolled a few metres before coming to rest.

'You OK?' said Jem, bending over the boy.

Alex opened one eye. 'Fine. Now . . . you and, sorry, don't know the other guy's name . . .'

'Pete,' said Jem.

'Dig yourselves in and get the paramedic to cover you up . . . then get the chopper well away from this valley, like we agreed.'

'Fine,' said Jem. And he ordered his crew to do exactly as the boy wanted. 'Use the downdraft for a few seconds,' he instructed the pilot though his helmet radio. 'See what you can do to blow away our footprints. The pilot thumbed up his agreement. A few minutes later he brought the chopper low enough to send fine powdery snow across their tracks before rising up and departing across the peaks. Soon it was out of sight and the beat of the rotors swiftly faded.

Gripping Alex's hand deep under the snow, Jem spoke, muffled: 'Twenty minutes, Alex, no more. I'm not having you die of exposure.'

From above, Dax Jones coasted the bumpy cold thermals and saw a boy, spread-eagled far below, half buried in snow. In spite of the helicopter pilot's best efforts, his astonishing falcon eyes could make out all the inconsistencies in this picture—but he was fairly sure that one panicked teleporter would not notice. Not until it was too late.

24

Granite stepped outside the bunker and raised his hand. Far down the beach, Olu looked up, not at the waving hand but at the prickling signal in his head which told him he was needed. He didn't know how Granite did this; in fact, he hadn't even thought much about it—certainly it had never occurred to him that telepathy was going on. Whenever he got the urge to port in to see the man, Granite always seemed to be expecting him. But Olu was not a deep thinker, so he did not much ponder on the mystery of this.

'Are you OK, Jacob?' asked Chambers, as soon as Marcus stepped out. 'You're not hurt?'

'No,' said Jacob. 'But they left Alex on the roof of a cable car, miles above the ground. He's been there at least two hours now, in the freezing cold.

We've *got* to get him back. Please make Granite do it! Please give him what he wants.'

Granite stepped back inside and beamed at them both.

'David,' he said, 'I'd like you to meet my very good friend—Olu.' And he pointed to an empty space in the middle of the brick hut. A second later the space was no longer empty as Olu teleported into it. The punch of crushed air made a hollow boom echo off the brick walls.

Chambers gasped, his eyes wide.

'Olu is your missing Cola,' explained Granite, patting the boy's shoulder. 'Did you even know he existed?'

Chambers stared at the boy. 'I did not know,' he said.

'Well, Olu's place is with me now,' said Granite, 'So you have no need to worry. The thing is, David, I can do a lot for the Colas. You did *know*, didn't you, that I was never an *ordinary* operative?' Chambers said nothing, but his eyes drifted to one side as if he was remembering something. 'You know that I have . . . some powers of my own. Oh no—I'm not a Cola; I didn't enter this world in the same way, but I have some extraordinary talents and I don't think they were the best kept secret while I was working for the British government. I mean, come *on* . . . some of the things I achieved for my country . . . you surely had to be asking *how.*'

'We knew you were different,' said Chambers. 'We also knew you couldn't be trusted. Which is why we stopped using your talents.'

'Well, maybe you should reconsider, because you are sitting on a time bomb. All those talented children . . . oh no . . . teenagers now and soon young men and young women, cloistered away together. You think you have one big happy family, do you? You think you can train and control and use them? But even now, while they're all minors and you still have their families on board, you're struggling. Admit it.'

'You know nothing of the Cola Project,' said Chambers.

'Oh dear,' chuckled Granite. 'Do you really believe that? I know far more about some of your charges than you or Paulina Sartre or any of the scientists do. I have met several of them, you know. The meetings have been most beneficial . . . to all parties.'

'I don't think Alex Teller is feeling much benefit right now,' said Chambers. 'And unless I see him right here in the next minute, this conversation is over.'

'Oh—Alex! Of course. Poor chap. Olu,' Chambers turned the boy to face him. 'Please go and collect Alex and bring him back here.'

Olu shrugged. 'OK,' he said, with a lazy grin. Jacob could tell, though, that the boy was not as relaxed as he appeared. Stress was emanating off him in almost visible waves, which Jacob had no difficulty in picking up. Did the boy *know* he was being manipulated and controlled? Jacob gnawed on his lower lip, his eyes falling quickly to Granite's silver ring, and quickly buried his new knowledge; he couldn't risk Granite picking up on it. He might need it . . . soon.

'Back in a mo,' said Olu, and vanished.

'I have a proposal,' said Granite. 'I want involvement. You need a back-up plan . . . and I can offer that. I can train and mentor your more troublesome Colas. I will never lose control. There will be no kidnaps, no disappearances, no trouble at all in keeping track of their whereabouts and their progress. You can keep the less problematic ones. I'm talking about those Colas that you're already starting to fear. Let me help before it's too late.

I can mould them into the UK's most incredible and most reliable assets. You know I can.'

Chambers said nothing, but he folded his arms and rested his back up against the wall. In his pocket the magnetic baubles from his desk sculpture crackled and Jacob suddenly opened his eyes wide as a long overdue message from Lisa landed in his mind.

Chambers has the balls, she said, in his head, as clearly as if she were in the room. She wasn't being rude. The balls in question were very small, black, round, and shiny. Six of them, in Chambers's pocket.

25

Olu arrived on the top of the cable car and the shock nearly sent him over the edge. He grabbed wildly for the metal struts above the empty roof and stared around in horror.

'ALEX!' he yelled, his heart racing. 'ALEX!' he yelled again, and this time his throat was so tight with misery the voice hardly made it out.

He hadn't wanted Granite to see it, but he had been feeling pretty bad. As the minutes wore on he had wished, fervently, that he'd chosen a better location to hold Alex. When he'd been in this valley only a few days ago it had been covered in grass and was as warm as an English meadow. Returning today he had been surprised to see all the snow—he hadn't expected it at this time of the year. Even so, he'd thought it would be fine; that Alex would only be there half an hour. But this whole thing had taken so long. He had been getting more and more anxious to return and collect the boy. He was hoping that after all this drama he and Alex—and maybe even Jacob—could still be friends. Last night's sleepover . . . the KFC and the chat and the laughs . . . had been so good. He'd realized how much he missed having friends. But Granite came first . . .

Now, though, everything had gone wrong. Horribly wrong. This was not the same as some anonymous security guard pegging out of a heart attack. Alex was just a *kid*—just like *him*. And now . . . he must be dead.

Olu crouched down; hanging on to the metal struts, and peered unhappily over the edge. He could see a tiny dark shape far down in the snow below. He closed his eyes. They were filling with tears and he was unable to bear that feeling. He did not *do* crying. Not for a very long time.

He knew he had to check. He had to go down there and be sure that it *was* Alex lying dead in the snow. He guessed it wasn't going to be a pretty sight after a fall from this height. He took a deep breath and ported off the cable car.

A second later he reappeared in the drift below. It was Alex all right, lying spread-eagled, half buried in a pile up of snow, as if he'd skidded into it at speed, pushing it up in a white wave.

'Oh mate,' said Olu, his voice thick. 'I didn't mean for this to happen.'

Alex's face was as still as carved stone . . . yet it looked pink. Olu frowned. Had he only *just* dropped? Had he missed the fall by seconds?

Then Alex opened his eyes.

Olu shouted out in shock.

'Olu . . . ?' The boy's voice came out rasping and thin. 'Olu . . . is that you?'

Olu skidded down, landing next to Alex on his knees. 'Alex! You're alive! Oh . . . man, I'm so sorry. You must be wrecked!'

'I'm OK,' said Alex. And he lifted one arm and one leg to prove it. 'I slid down a lot of the way . . . from further up the slope.'

'No *way!*' said Olu. 'Nobody could survive a fall like that!'

'I'm a Cola,' said Alex. 'We're tough. Superpowers . . . remember?'

Olu stared at him, fascinated. 'Really? You mean . . . we can, like, heal ourselves?'

'Well . . . sometimes,' grunted Alex. 'Or we're harder to break. I think my other leg's broken though. You have to take me back to Jacob. *Please!*'

Olu hesitated, looking troubled. This was not the way it was meant to play out . . . not at all. He was meant to bounce back to Granite and Jacob and this guy, Chambers, with Alex a bit cold and shivery, but none the worse for his ordeal. Porting back a kid with a broken leg and . . . who knows . . . maybe internal injuries, was going to mess up the scene a bit.

Alex grabbed his hand. 'I'll be OK,' he croaked. 'Take me back—and then Jacob will know what to do. If I stay here in the cold I'll die. Olu—please—be my friend. Don't let me die.'

'OK,' said Olu, putting his other hand on top of Alex's.

Far inside the snowdrift Alex clenched Jem's hand. And Jem clenched Pete's hand.

And three seconds later all four of them teleported out of the valley.

'Thing is, David,' went on Granite, in an oh-so-reasonable tone. 'If you *don't* want my help, it's not really a deal breaker for me.'

Chambers raked his fingers through his close-cropped hair and tried to keep his mind out of freefall. He had already worked this out, but hearing the man actually say it aloud opened up a whole new chasm of trouble in his world.

'As you've discovered, with Olu's help I can pluck all your more interesting charges away. One by one, as soon as I'm ready for them. I would prefer them to come to me willingly, of course, but it will only be a matter of time before they understand that I have not kidnapped them, but delivered them . . . from an institutionalized future of serfdom to the British security services. I will offer them choices. And I am confident they will make the right choices.'

Chambers closed his eyes, suddenly incredibly weary. There was no answer to this. Would he have to negotiate with this man? Get him involved? How? When he could *never* trust him. The Cola Project was far from perfect, he knew that . . . but at least it wasn't being run by one power-crazed fanatic.

'So . . . what is it to be?' asked Granite. 'Or shall we just wait for Olu to pop back with Alex? Then you can set your mind at rest and start to talk.' Granite gazed around the room, flicking his eyes past Jacob with little interest. He saw no threat in the boy at all and, clearly, had no further use for him. 'I do wonder what's keeping them . . .'

Then there was a powerful thud as Olu returned. With far more than anyone had bargained for.

26

At first it was chaos. The small brick hut suddenly filled to capacity with Olu, Alex, and two well-built SAS-trained operatives. The displaced air punched and sucked and popped in everyone's ears and cracks opened up along the ceiling and the far wall, sending small showers of sand and brick dust down on top of their heads.

The men hit the floor, but they didn't flop, dazed and disorientated. As Jem had explained to Alex while they were waiting under the snow, he and Pete had undergone rigorous training as fighter pilots in the RAF. They had tolerated intense G-force and weightlessness time and again, and were well able to cope. Alex had also checked that neither of them had any metal plates in their heads or gadgets in their bodies which might blow apart and kill them; they didn't.

As Olu gave a yell of horror—'I DIDN'T KNOW! He TRICKED me!'—Jacob dashed forward and grabbed Alex away from him.

The brothers gave each other a rough hug. 'You OK?' demanded Jacob.

'Freezing cold!' muttered Alex, his teeth chattering, 'But I'll be fine.'

Chambers and Granite were both flattened up against the same wall, their eyes wide with amazement. The torch was kicked over and the light split and splintered around so many bodies.

'Sir!' yelled Jem, clapping astonished eyes on his boss in a stray beam of light. 'Are you injured?'

'No,' called back Chambers. 'Get Jacob and Alex out of here!'

'With respect, sir,' called back Jem. 'Not without you.'

'Time for us to go, Olu,' called out Granite, and in a shard of torchlight Jacob saw him twisting the ring upright on his finger and moving to reach Olu, on the far side of the hut.

Jacob had no time to explain anything to anyone. Lisa's message was clear. He had to act now. 'Granite! Stay where you are!' he yelled, in an exact replica of Olu's voice. In the flashing light of the grounded torch, Granite paused, looking confused. And this gave Jacob enough time to dart across and thrust his hand into Chambers's jacket pocket, pulling out the cluster of six magnetite spheres.

'I didn't say that!' yelled Olu.

'Granite—stay still!' yelled Jacob again, in Olu's voice. Then he threw himself across the room and grabbed the boy, holding one magnetite ball directly against his skin. He felt Olu try to port away—felt the hot energy bounce through him . . . and fail.

'Get OFF!' bawled Olu. More light filled the room now as the operatives pulled out their own torches. In the flashes Jacob saw Olu's terrified face as he pinned the boy to the wall, struggling desperately not to lose contact between his own skin, Olu's skin, and the magnetite between. And now Granite pitched in, trying to wrench Jacob away from his protégé. The skirmish ended up on the floor and here, in the confusion, Jacob took a chance. Wresting one hand free he swiftly poked one small magnetite ball into one of the neat plaits along Olu's scalp. Was this close enough to the boy's scalp? He really hoped so.

As the special ops guys pulled Granite back, Jacob got up and handed each of them a magnetite sphere. 'Keep it against your skin!' he ordered. 'And then Olu can't take you.'

'GO, Olu!' yelled Granite. 'Port away!'

But Olu, scrambling to his feet, unaware of the bead of magnetite tight against his scalp, yelled back 'You're stopping me! Let me go.'

'I am not stopping you!' shouted back Granite. Within the iron grip of Jem, Jacob saw Granite glance down at the ring . . . yes, the dark orb in it was twisted into the upright position, held clear of skin contact by its silver setting. Earlier it had been twisted down; set to 'stay'. Now it was on 'depart'.

'He has been controlling you, though, Olu,' Jacob said. 'He's been using a mineral . . . an ore called magnetite. It's like Kryptonite for you, although I doubt he's ever told you about it, has he?'

'What does he mean?' asked Olu, staring at Granite.

'Not now, Olu!' grunted Granite. 'Later!'

'But he's not the only one who's got it, *now*,' said Jacob. 'Anyone can get magnetite. They put it in jewellery, in gadgets . . . even in executive desk toys.' He held up the three remaining baubles from Chambers's pocket and then gave one to Chambers and Alex. 'Don't let go of them,' he said. 'We're all covered now, Olu,' he said. 'You can't port us. The magnetite makes contact through skin. Granite has it in that ring on his left hand— isolated in the silver setting. Whenever he needs to stop you porting him he just twists the ring so the magnetite swings down under his knuckle and he can press it to his palm, unseen. And I guess he presses it against *you* whenever he wants to stop you porting away.'

'Ignore him, Olu!' commanded Granite. 'GO! Leave me!'

'But . . . I can't!' Olu's eyes rolled wildly in the dim light from the doorway. He turned to run but Pete stepped across and blocked his exit.

'Jacob—Alex!' cried Olu, turning to them with a wretched expression. 'Tell them to let me *go*! You'll never see me again. C'mon . . . Jake! We had a good time, didn't we? I never wanted anyone to get hurt, mate . . . just let me *go*!'

'Can't do that,' said Jacob. 'Sorry . . . *mate.*'

The air sucked and punched endlessly as Olu

vainly flexed his power, making their ears pop and whine with the twisted pressure, scattering more fine brick dust and sand from the cracks in the roof and walls, but still Olu remained locked to his location.

Held firm by Jem, Granite said, quietly, to Chambers, 'Don't let him go on so. It's not good for him.'

Olu didn't look good. His eyes were wide and glassy as he endlessly tried and failed to port. Beads of sweat appeared on his skin. A small red line of blood began to trickle from one nostril. Jacob, in spite of everything, shared a thought with Alex: *It'll be like caging a wild animal, won't it? He'll die.*

Alex sent back, *Yeah . . .* and shared a mental image of Olu in an underground prison, wrapped in chains of magnetite. *But I don't know what we can do about it now. What happens next?*

What happened next took everyone by surprise.

The roof fell in.

27

Nearly a century of pressure from the weight of sand and vegetation would not normally have been a problem for the structure . . . but the laws of physics were being shaken down by Olu's attempts to port. They had barely noticed the showers of sand and brick dust getting thicker. Suddenly, with a great thump, the structure collapsed. Bricks and sand flopped down like a lead blanket and everyone was flattened to the floor.

Except Olu. He was knocked sideways but fell outwards, through the doorway. The outer wall, strengthened by the concrete lintel above the door, held up and he was only struck across his shins by a few rolling bricks.

He scrambled to his feet and ran, panic flooding through him. He had not felt this afraid since the days with his dad, before he could get away. As soon as he was down at the water's edge he tried to port, but nothing happened. The panic intensified. He *had* to get back! Back to the green pool and the house in the Dominican mountains. He needed to get away!

Instead, he ran. And, looking back, he realized he was not alone. The collapse had not crushed them all to death. Two figures were haring across the beach towards him—Jacob and Alex. And now a third figure began to run after them—tall and lean. That had to be Chambers.

Olu ran flat out, heading for higher ground. He felt, somehow, if he could just get higher, his panic would ease and he would be able to teleport again. He just needed to get up high and slow his breathing and focus. His power would come back—it *would*!

'We have to catch him!' panted Jacob, doing his best to ignore the blood that was running into his eyes from a cut across his forehead. 'If we don't he'll find Granite again somehow and port him away . . . Then . . . who knows what they'll do next?!'

'Why hasn't he . . . gone already?' Alex was limping along beside his brother. His legs were horribly grazed and his upper arms would be black and blue from the impact of all the bricks. Some instinct had made him raise his arms, saving him from concussion. The other guys—Jem and Pete— seemed to be OK too. The bricks had not fallen with enough velocity to knock them out. Decades of thick weed roots had held a large part of the ground above in place. Granite, though, had been laid out cold on the floor.

'He's still got a magnetite ball on him . . . in his hair,' replied Jacob. 'He doesn't know.'

'Wait!' bellowed Chambers, gaining on them from behind. 'Do NOT engage with him!' His glasses were broken and abandoned and he had stripped off and dumped his jacket, which was heavy with blood from a wound he'd sustained behind one ear. He had jammed the magnetite ball inside his watch strap, tight against his wrist. His fury at this hash-up was driving him faster than the boys. He must catch them before they caught Olu. The boy's power might come back at any moment. He could not *bear* to see them all vanish before his eyes.

But now Olu had reached the top of the cliff path, and suddenly he stopped, swaying gently in the warm afternoon breeze. He turned to look down at the brothers on the path below.

'Don't waste your time,' he called. 'I can port again now.'

He's bluffing, Jacob sent to Alex, *There's still magnetite in his hair—or he'd already be gone.*

But Olu held up a small glinting dark ball. 'Nice try, Jake! In the hair, eh? Clever!'

They scrambled on up the path, kicking away small avalanches of sand. Jacob couldn't work out why Olu was still there, waiting for them.

'You should come with me!' called Olu. 'Come on! You know you want to, really. Come with me and live your life free! We can go anywhere and do anything! We'll be a team!'

'You're not,' puffed Alex, 'a team player.'

'I can learn!' pleaded Olu, as they reached the grassy top of the narrow promontory which stretched far out into the sea, meeting the returning tide. 'And look . . . what have you got to look forward to back at your high security college? They'll never let you go, you know. This is probably the last bit of freedom you're ever going to taste. Don't go back! Come with me!'

He backed away from them as Jacob and Alex

approached more slowly, staggering slightly over a high tussock of grass. Behind him was a long drop to the rocks below. They could hear the sea crashing against it.

'We have friends at our college,' said Jacob, clenching his magnetite in his palm. 'And family who come and stay and people who look after us—people we trust.'

'What—like Chambers?' scoffed Olu. 'You think you can trust *Chambers*? What does *he* care about you? He just works for the government. He's not worried about your welfare—he only cares about how you can be *used*. He doesn't give a monkey's about you!'

Jacob knew that shreds of Olu's words were true. But he also remembered Chambers back in his office—that odd, unexpected, compassionate hug. Chambers *did* care. He was certain of it.

'Come with me!' called Olu once more. Alex suddenly realized how lonely he was. It was leeching out of him. Olu was so, so alone. What else would induce him to stay when he could be, even now, back in the green pool, back in his mountainside retreat—anywhere else at all?

But before either of them could speak, a figure launched itself from over the edge of the cliff and knocked Olu sideways. Chambers had climbed stealthily up another path. He landed hard on the boy, disabling him with shocking ease, pulling his arms up behind him and pushing his face into the grass. Chambers's magnetite ball was now wedged in his fingers and pressed hard against the nape of Olu's neck.

'Alex—Jacob—I need your help,' grunted Chambers, as Olu writhed and yowled with fury, hopelessly pinned down now. The ruthless soldier inside Chambers was still, clearly, very very active. 'Get over here! Now!' called Chambers. 'Get your magnetite out. Help me!'

They moved towards the man and boy, uncertain and shocked.

'Jacob—press your magnetite to his skin while I flip him over,' commanded Chambers. "We mustn't lose contact or he'll be gone.'

Jacob did so, holding the small dark sphere against Olu's side as Chambers wrestled the boy round onto his back and pinned his wrists back together in a vice-like grip, while pressing one knee onto his chest.

'I'm sorry,' he told his captive. 'I don't want it to be like this. But you leave me no choice. Alex!

I need your magnetite now.' He gestured with his free hand and Alex approached. As he got closer to the huddle on the cliff top he saw Chambers pinch Olu's nose tight shut.

'What—what are you doing?' asked Alex, horror sweeping over him in waves.

'Quick!' said Chambers. 'I need it now. This is the only way.' His finger and thumb continued to pinch Olu's nostrils shut and the boy was forced to breathe through his mouth.

Alex realized what the plan was. Chambers was going to make Olu *swallow* the magnetite.

'I don't think . . .' he began. 'I mean . . . I think I've lost mine. In the chase.'

Chambers gritted his teeth. 'OK—Jacob. Please—hand me yours!'

Jacob, still kneeling at Olu's side, glanced at his brother. *Are we . . . are we going to do this?*

No, said Alex. *This is all wrong.*

But the decision was made for them. Taking advantage of the confusion, Olu suddenly struck out and rolled out from under Chambers's hold.

Three seconds later he was at the very edge of the cliff.

The magnetite balls had spun away into the

thick, high grass. Jacob and Alex should have been scrabbling for them but they didn't move. Chambers was on his feet and walking slowly towards Olu.

'It's too late. I'm going now,' said Olu. 'You can't stop me.'

'So go,' said Chambers.

But Olu didn't. He just stared at Chambers. 'You've got no magic ball bearings now, have you?' he said.

'Seems not,' said Chambers, still getting closer.

'So what is it . . . you want to come with me?' said Olu, and a gleam flickered across his eyes.

'Chambers!' warned Jacob. 'Don't touch him.'

'Olu—it's not too late to make everything better,' said Chambers. 'You could come with us—back to Cola Club—be with Jacob and Alex. Have friends— support—a *life* . . .'

'You call that a life?!' snorted Olu. 'I'm the one who's got the life! I'm free! Hey—I know—you all come with me! C'mon! Let's all link hands and I'll take you to Rio for the carnivals! To Australia for some surfing! What do you say?'

'Not these two,' said Chambers. 'They've done enough travelling. But you can take me. Come on, Olu. Show me your world.'

And he clasped Olu's shoulder.

'Where do you think he'd like to go?' asked Olu, grinning at Jacob and Alex as he suddenly wrapped his arms around Chambers's shoulders. 'Niagara Falls? Reckon he'll have time to see it before his brain pops?'

'Get away from him, Chambers!' yelled Jacob. 'If you port anywhere with him you'll die! You've got metal in your head!'

Chambers looked baffled, and then realization seemed to strike and he began to wrestle Olu off him. But Olu leaped onto his back like a child. 'OK—let's go! You might get to see the Grand Canyon before your head explodes.'

'Olu—don't do it,' Alex pleaded. 'You don't want anyone else on your conscience.'

'What makes you think I *have* a conscience?!' said Olu, with a cracked laugh.

'Please, Olu—NO!' begged Alex. 'Don't do this. You've never killed anyone deliberately—I've always believed that. You don't want to start now.'

Olu's grin wobbled. 'OK, maybe I don't. I'll let him go if he lets me go.'

He jumped down and stepped away while Chambers looked from him to the brothers, shaking his head in defeat. It was a stalemate. And yet he had one more try.

'You can still come with us,' said Chambers, wiping sweat off his upper lip. 'I mean it. We'll look after you. You can't trust Granite. He's only using you for his own ends.'

'And you wouldn't?' asked Olu.

Chambers said nothing.

Olu shook his head and turned away, gazing over the drop. He clenched his fists several times and when he turned back his mouth was twisted and there were tears running down his face. 'I still can't port,' he mumbled. 'Something's gone wrong. You—you've ruined it!' He stared accusingly at Jacob. 'That stuff—that *stuff*!' His heels were on the very edge.

He locked his dark eyes with Alex's, and Alex found himself inside the boy's head. Invited. *I'm sorry,* said Olu. *We had a good time last night, didn't we? Yeah? For a while?*

Alex nodded. It had been good. For a while.

It was the best time. You know . . . having mates again. Olu squeezed his eyes shut tight and scrubbed at them, sniffing hard. *Now I think I have to die. Please . . . Alex . . . just . . . let me stay dead, will you?*

Then he tipped backwards.

Two seconds later there was a splash, just audible above the surge of the sea.

Chambers, Alex and Jacob ran to the edge of the cliff and peered over, aghast. Below was a swirling mass of grey-green water, pounding the rocks. One of Olu's trainers bobbed on the water. Of the boy himself there was no sign.

'What happened?' asked Chambers, dropping to his knees and leaning out, appalled. 'Did he port? Did he fall?'

'He fell,' said Alex. His throat was tight and his voice came out full of tears. 'The magnetite . . . must have affected him more than we realized. Maybe it was too much. I think . . . I think we killed him.'

28

Jem was beside himself when they got back to the collapsed hut. He and Pete had crawled out, injured but not down, and then gone back in to drag Marcus Croft out and secure him properly.

But Marcus Croft, or Granite—or whoever he really was—had gone.

'*Damn*!' Jem pounded a fist against the old fortification and then stepped quickly away as the wall cracked. 'We followed tracks across the sand . . . but there's nothing. Nothing.'

David Chambers landed his right palm heavily on Jem's shoulder. 'Let it go, Jem. Let's get back.'

They all piled into the 4x4 and headed back to the airfield. Chambers called in some details—as much as he knew—to Control and two hours later they were all back at Fenton Lodge, exhausted.

Chambers passed the debrief duty to Control. For several hours he, Jacob, Alex, Jem and Pete told and retold their story. It was hard to piece together, and even harder to believe, but evidence was showing up—the icy swimming trunks in Iceland, Dax Jones and the pilot's account when they returned from the Alps, Jacob's mouthed Cola emergency message to the security camera in the London bank, which had now found its way to Control—'Tell Chambers—it's a code 46!' There *was* such a thing as a teleporter. Nobody could argue.

Then they all took themselves away to what relief they could find. For Alex and Jacob that was simple enough, Chambers hoped. They had saved each other, one way or another. They had, Chambers guessed, saved *him* too—from a hideous compromise with Marcus Croft. But it was hard to feel much joy when he thought of how the day had ended. For Olu to throw himself off a cliff rather than come to Cola Club?

Chambers had a shower in his private quarters—a cottage set high on the fells above the college, but well within the closely guarded perimeter. He drank tea and ate toast. He took himself to bed and lay, too exhausted even to sleep. And one feeble question arced across his mind like a flare from a distant planet. He had thought he'd put a stop to it but now it was back to haunt his soul.

What happened to Louisa?

29

Jacob struggled far more than Chambers had guessed. As relieved as he was to be back at the lodge with his brother, safe and sound, in the early hours he was still wide awake.

Go to SLEEP! sent Alex, a dim shape in the next bed.

Jacob continued to stare into the dark, a bitter shame gnawing at his insides.

Alex sat up and switched on the lamp. 'Look— you had no choice. Chambers knew that. He doesn't blame you.'

'I know,' mumbled Jacob. 'But I just can't forget what I said to him, pretending to be this girl . . . you know, this girl he loved and . . . then . . . got accused of murdering and . . .'

Alex got up with a sigh and stood on the floor

in his pyjamas. 'Come on,' he said. 'We're going to see Lisa.'

If he hadn't been so tired, Chambers would never have agreed to it . . . but he was exhausted and brought so low by the events of the day before that he gave in.

And so only a day later, he and the Teller Brothers were back on the beach—with Lisa. Jem had come too, as security—a flimsy amount of it for a Cola outing, but Chambers could not bear any more. Cola Project teams were busy anyway, still combing the area, seeking a body of a teenage boy.

Much of the collapsed brick hut had been cleared away while the area was thoroughly searched for clues of Marcus Croft's disappearance, but about a metre of the walls still stood, and here, in the bright sunlight, Chambers could see chalk marks. Drawings Louisa had made twenty years ago. 'There,' he said—pointing.

Lisa knelt down and pressed her fingers to the pale blue doodle of . . . a dragonfly, she realized, as soon as she made contact. She closed her eyes and sent: *Come on. Now's the time. Louisa!*

As Jem roamed watchfully nearby, Chambers sat down on the remains of the opposite wall and tried not to let a flutter of hope pass through him. Louisa was dead. He was sure of it now.

Jacob, a short distance away with his brother, glanced across to the beach and the promontory from which Olu had fallen. *I still can't believe he did that,* he sent to Alex.

His brother turned and looked too. *Can't you?* he replied.

Well, it was a hell of a risk, wasn't it? Jacob shuddered. *And we don't know whether he pulled it off, do we? He might really have drowned.*

Nah—he's a great swimmer, said Alex. *And anyway, I'm sure he ported away while he was under the water.*

Jacob rubbed his face, still tired. *He was cleverer than he looked, wasn't he?*

Alex nodded, staring out to sea. *Yep. He could have just vanished, but he worked out that if he seemed to be dead there would be less chance of the Project bothering to catch him. He asked me to let him stay 'dead'. Did you hear that bit?*

Yeah, I heard, Jacob nodded at Chambers who was intently watching Lisa and waiting for news. *But do you think we should tell him?*

228

What's the point? said Alex. *They suspect anyway, because of the way Granite disappeared. And . . . the way Chambers was trying to stuff magnetite down his throat . . .* He shivered. *I know Olu was wrong. But getting him back to Fenton Lodge and locking him down, maybe for ever . . . destroying his freedom . . . is that right?*

No, said Jacob. *Not that he didn't deserve it, for what he put you through. But I guess I would have done the same . . . I just hope we don't end up regretting it.*

Lisa stood and walked across to Chambers. She rested one hand on his shoulder and smiled gently. 'You knew she was dead, didn't you?' she said. Chambers nodded. 'It's just *how* that messes you up,' she went on. 'But it's OK. I know how.' She sat down next to him and took his hand, as if she were Mia. A gesture most unlike Lisa. 'It was an accident,' she said. 'Louisa was hit by a car, on the lane behind the park. She died instantly—really didn't know a thing about it. And the driver—well, he ran at first. And then he came back and picked up her body and put it in the boot—and then drove the car to a remote lake—and let it roll in. She says he was crying all the way there. I can show you where she is.'

Chambers nodded, wave after wave of emotion

hitting him. Grief, of course, but also . . . tremendous relief.

'These days they'd have found traces of her, I'm sure,' went on Lisa. 'But back then they weren't so clever. A shame for you and her family. Twenty years of misery. I'm really sorry, Mr Chambers.'

'Is she . . . where she is now, I mean . . . is she . . .?' he began.

Lisa smiled. 'She says to say "hi",' she grinned. 'And she'll see you again one day. And also . . . *The kindest one holds the flame.*' Lisa shrugged. 'That mean anything to you?'

'Um—no, I don't think so,' said Chambers. 'But—thank you. Very, very much.'

30

Mia hated the magnetite bracelet. Everyone was wearing them until the scientists worked out a more sophisticated way of protecting them all from teleportation. Something about it made her feel sick. She took it off and buried it in a drawer.

'Good girl,' said Spook, when she confessed this to him, during a walk through the woods. 'I got shot of mine too. It's just one more shackle as far as I can see.' He turned and touched her face again, his eyes soft on hers. 'I always knew you were stronger than you looked. But they'll start locking us down soon . . . you'll see. I will probably be first.'

'What do you mean? Nobody's locking you down!' Mia's violet eyes widened in dismay.

'They will,' said Spook. 'I disappeared too, remember, but they can't find out anything from

231

me. They don't trust me. Wait. You'll see. And when it happens . . .' He pulled her into a tight embrace, stroking her hair. 'Help me.'

'I will,' said Mia. 'I will.'

Ali Sparkes is a journalist and BBC broadcaster who chucked in the safe job to go dangerously freelance and try her hand at writing comedy scripts. Her first venture was as a comedy columnist on *Woman's Hour* and later on *Home Truths*. Not long after, she discovered her real love was writing children's fiction.

Ali grew up adoring adventure stories about kids who mess about in the woods and still likes to mess about in the woods herself whenever possible. She lives with her husband and two sons in Southampton, England. Check out www.alisparkes.com for the latest news on Ali's forthcoming books.

**Look out for the final book in the
mind-blowing UNLEASHED series**

THE BURNING BEACH

**Ultimate powers. Deadly secrets.
Impossible choices.**

Mia can't remember how she ended up unconscious on a
deserted beach. All she knows is that something terrible
has happened—and that *she* is somehow responsible.
Realizing she can never go back to her old life, Mia
vanishes off the radar. But with enemies closing in all
around her, there's no way she can stay hidden for ever . . .

OUT JANUARY 2014